SHAKA II

Tarikian, TARK Classic Fiction, Arc Manor, Arc Manor Classic Reprints, Phoenix Pick, Phoenix Rider, Manor Thrift, The Stellar Guild Series, The Phoenix Science Fiction Classics Series, Phoenix Pick Booklets and logos associated with those imprints are trademarks or registered trademarks of Arc Manor, LLC, Rockville, Maryland. All other trademarks and trademarked names are properties of their respective owners.

This book is presented as is, without any warranties (implied or otherwise) as to the accuracy of the production, text or translation.

ISBN: 978-1-61242-258-9

www.PhoenixPick.com
Great Science Fiction at Great Prices

Published by Phoenix Pick
an imprint of Arc Manor
P. O. Box 10339
Rockville, MD 20849-0339
www.ArcManor.com

SHAKA II

MIKE RESNICK

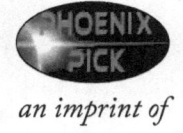

an imprint of

Rockville, Maryland

PROLOGUE

BEFORE SHAKA, WE WERE NO MORE important than the ants on the ground.

In 1816 AD, Zululand was the size of a very large farm, extending almost two miles in every direction from the central *kraal*. The dominant tribes in southern Africa were the Mtebele and the Shona.

Then came Shaka, who claimed the kingship of the Zulus. He reigned for only twelve years, yet when he was assassinated in 1828, the Zulus controlled an empire far larger than the country of France, and more than two million men had died opposing the creation of that empire.

The Zulus remained South Africa's dominant tribe for the rest of the century, but one by one they lost their wars against the British and the Boers, and suddenly found themselves dominated within their own homeland by the Xhosa.

Seventy-five years after Shaka's death, our primacy was gone, and for another century we were dominated, in turn, by white men, brown men, and black men. The white men controlled our land and the Indians controlled our economy, and when they were finally removed from power, that power was claimed not by the Zulus, but by the Xhosa.

For years then, for decades, for more than two centuries, even after Man moved out into space and onto other worlds, every time a baby boy was born to a Zulu family, his parents and relatives and neighbors would gather around and stare at him, wondering: Are you the One? Are you finally the One who will restore our former glory, who will reclaim what was Shaka's and what was ours?

And one day, though of course we didn't know it at the time, he was among us.

1.

His name was Robert ole Buthelezi, and there didn't seem to be anything special about him as a small child. Quite the contrary, in fact. It took him four years to speak, eight to read. A lonely child whose father ignored him and whose mother worked long hours and turned her children over to the care of various relatives, he became totally self-sufficient at an early age. He was a clumsy youngster, and sometimes when he ran his knees would give out and he'd go sprawling. He had no interest in school, and his grades reflected that.

On the whole he was an unimpressive child, with nothing much to recommend him. I say "nothing much" because there were a few things that stand out in my memory.

When he would fall, or otherwise hurt himself, he never cried or asked for help. Not once.

When he fell sick—and he was sicker than most children— he never complained about the treatment, and some of those treatments would have had other children screaming in fear or pain or both.

He made terrible blunders in his classrooms. But he never made the same one twice. He didn't act like an earnest young man who was compelled to learn, but he retained everything he saw and heard. Everything.

He was without compassion. The suffering of a neighbor's pet, or a relative in a hospital, left him cold. But if he had no compassion for others, he had none for himself, either; self-pity was simply not in his lexicon. It wasn't that he was stoic, but rather that he simply ignored discomfort and even pain. One got the distinct impression that pain, even his own, simply didn't interest him.

I remember the day—he had just entered his teens—that three older boys who didn't like his arrogant attitude lay in wait and pounced on him. He fought back as best he could, but they left him lying in the street, barely conscious, blood pouring from a dozen wounds. He finally got shakily to his feet, refused all medical aid, and decided that he had to become stronger. Beginning the next morning, long before he was healed, he began running five miles before breakfast. His feet bled, and he passed out from exhaustion, but when he was revived he continued on his journey until the five miles were completed. He repeated the procedure every morning, and one day we began to notice that he was covering the ground at a rapid pace without ever taking a deep breath.

He began swimming in the ocean, unmindful of sharks, and built his strength and stamina through force of will, much as he had with his running. He never asked for company, but if anyone wanted to run or swim with him, he never objected, though he would soon leave them far behind.

After he had spent half a year building up his body, he called out the three older boys who had beaten him up. I didn't see the fight, but I know that all three boys were rushed to the intensive care unit after it was over.

He vanished before the authorities could find him, and since we didn't hear from him for the next ten years, most people assumed he was dead. I was one of the ones who didn't. There was something about him, even as a boy, some aura that said whatever else he might become, he would never be a victim.

Soon people forgot all about him, and the cycles of life continued. Day followed night, summer followed spring, the long rains followed the parched dry weather, and all was as it should be.

And then one day I heard a single loud knock at my door. I walked over and opened it—and found myself facing Robert ole Buthelezi.

"Aren't you going to invite me in, my brother?" he said, an amused smile on his face.

2.

WE WERE NOT BROTHERS IN the truest sense. My name is John Madondo, and my Zulu name, which I chose not to use, was John ole Buthelezi, which means, literally, "John, son of Buthelezi." Robert is also a son of Buthelezi, but we did not have the same mother, and in fact Buthelezi never married either of them, which is not the shameful event that it would be in Western society. Many Zulus chose not to marry, and a number of Zulu men had multiple wives. In fact, we had four other half-brothers and three half-sisters that we knew about, and never doubted that there were others as well.

"Come in," I replied when I had recovered from my surprise at seeing him. "Many thought you were dead, but somehow I knew you were alive."

"There were days I would have bet money on the other side," he said, walking over and sitting on my favorite lounge chair. His tall frame made it look like a child's chair. "You left to become a teacher when I was still a child. Are you teaching now?"

"Yes," I said. "I came back to Natal after receiving my degree."

"It is a land with no present and less future."

"All the more reason to educate those who must live here," I answered.

"It is good that you should think so," he said, looking around at my simple furnishings, "because clearly you are not growing wealthy from your profession." He paused. "Have you any tea?"

"Tea, coffee, beer, whatever you like," I said.

"Tea," he answered.

I went to the kitchen, made the tea, poured two cups, and returned with it. "Where have you been?" I asked.

"Away," is all he answered.

"Johannesburg?" I suggested.

A smile. "There is more to the world than South Africa. Men have reached the stars, and you still live in a four-room hovel and teach children who dress in rags."

"The rags do not define them," I said.

"Are you satisfied with your work?" he asked. Then: "With your life?"

"They need me," I replied. "I just wish I made more of a difference."

"Perhaps someday you will," he said.

"Perhaps." I secretly doubted it, and decided it was time to change the subject. "What has brought you back?" I asked.

"The world—the *real* world—thinks that we are a backwater, barely worthy of their notice. If we are to reclaim our former glory, to stride across the planet like gods, there is much to be done, and I have no time to waste."

I expected him to smile, or chuckle, to do something, *anything*, to show me that he was joking, but his expression never changed.

"*Are* we to stride across the planet like gods?" I asked at last.

"Oh, yes," he said with certainty. "That much is written in the Book of Fate."

"I have never seen that," I said.

"You have flawed vision," he replied.

"Who wrote this passage that I have not seen?" I continued.

"I am writing it even as we speak."

"Have you a place to stay?" I asked.

"No," he answered. "I had hoped to stay with my older brother."

"And have you any money?"

He reached into a pocket and pulled out some coins. "Less than a rand."

"No luggage?"

"I travel light."

"So you are homeless, destitute, without a rand to your name, and with only the clothing on your back," I said. "And you are going to bring us back the primacy we possessed when Shaka walked the land five centuries ago."

He stared at me for a long moment. "Will you stand in my way?"

"No," I said. "Why should I?"

He smiled. "You see? I have one acolyte already."

"I am *not* an acolyte," I said firmly. "I am an unhostile observer, nothing more."

He shrugged. "Semantics."

"So," I said, "will you establish your kingdom here in my living room, and eventually conquer the dining room and kitchen?"

He stared at me so silently and coldly that for a moment I thought he was going to get to his feet and attack me. Then he shrugged.

"You can join me now," he said, "or you can join me later, when you have no choice in the matter. But do not ever make fun of me again."

It was a simple statement, simply delivered, but for the first time in my adult life I was frightened.

"I apologize, Robert," I said. "Seriously, what *are* your plans?"

"There is to be an election next month," he said.

"You are mistaken," I told him. "The President has another year and a half to serve."

He stared at me again and I fell silent. "It is a minor office," he said. "Clerk of Records in Natal. But I must start somewhere, and I need not think about the presidency for another year."

I had thought I knew him, but I was amazed by the audacity of his ambition—not running for Clerk of Records, but planning on running for the presidency in a mere eighteen months. I was afraid if I commented on it, I would receive another hate-filled glare and sullen silence, so I decided to change the subject.

"Where have you been for the past decade?" I asked.

"In the world of the *ibhunu*," he said. In the Zulu language, calling a white man *ibhunu* is like calling a black man *nigger* in English.

"There are very few white men left here," I said. "Where did you go?"

"Europe," he said. "Then America. Then farther afield."

"How much farther can you go than America?" I asked.

"Just as there is a world beyond South Africa, there is a solar system beyond the world, and a galaxy beyond the solar system."

"You've been out there?" I asked, impressed.

"I spent four years in the American Space Fleet," he replied.

"Did you see action against…against whatever they were, those things that attacked our colonies on Io and Ganymede?"

He nodded. "They had technology that was far superior to ours. Of course, we have it now."

"How did you defeat them?" I asked. "I know that for a year all the news coming from the front was bad, and then one day it was over and we were victorious."

"They were fools," he said, a look of contempt on his face. "They sent a signal asking for more munitions. We tracked the signal and wiped out their home world. Their remaining ships surrendered."

"Where *was* their home world?" I asked. "Most of the experts thought it must circle Centauri."

"It was the sixth planet circling Wolf 359," he answered.

I frowned. "That can't be. Wolf is a Class M star. Nothing can live in orbit around a Class M star."

"Nothing does *now*," he said meaningfully. "You should not be so quick to believe European and American astronomers. What we killed would give you nightmares for the rest of your life. You should be grateful such things can't evolve on a Class G star."

"Did they give *you* nightmares?" I asked.

He almost looked amused. "I am not like you," he said.

It wouldn't be long before I learned just how unlike me he was.

3.

When he was a child, he always found a way to get what he wanted. He never cried, never screamed, never threatened—but somehow things would always work out for him. His methods were subtle. The children who stood in his way never showed up cowed or beaten...but twice they never showed up again at all.

Robert told me that his opponent for the office he wanted was Hector ole Kunene, a nondescript little civil servant who was being given the job as payment for his loyalty to the party over the years. Both sides agreed that he deserved the office, and he was running unopposed.

"Will you run as an independent, then?" I asked.

He shook his head. "I have a party."

"Oh?"

"The Zulu Party."

I frowned. "There *is* no Zulu Party," I said.

"There is now."

"Shall I assume you are its only member?" I asked with a smile.

"You would be mistaken," he said seriously. "You are also a member."

"I am?" I said, surprised.

He nodded. "I must repay you for the generosity you have shown me tonight," he said. "You will come to Ulundi with me and be my assistant."

"I have a job and a home right here."

"Leave them," he said with a look of contempt. "Come with me and you shall be rewarded beyond your expectations."

"I am happy where I am," I said. "I love the children I teach, and Ulundi is a crowded, filthy, dangerous city."

That amused smile again. "Do you think Ulundi is my destination? It is merely a brief stop along the way, nothing more."

"Pretoria?" I asked, amazed at his raw ambition.

"Soon."

"And beyond that?"

"We shall see."

"Every twenty years or so someone envisions himself as the new Shaka," I said. "Yet thirty-five million Zulus are still living in Natal Province, and we are still without power of any kind—military, political, or economic. Why should anyone believe you are the One we have been waiting for?"

"I do not claim to be anyone's reincarnation," he said. "And as a Zulu, you should know that his name was Tchaka, not Shaka, which is the Europeans' corruption of it."

"You still haven't answered my question," I persisted. "Why should we believe in you? What have you done thus far to inspire confidence?"

"I am just beginning," he said.

"And have accomplished nothing."

He reached into a pocket and tossed something to me. "Here is the nothing I have been accomplished."

They were medals. More to the point, they included three of the highest medals the American Space Fleet had to offer.

"This is very impressive," I said. "I had no idea. We heard nothing of this here in Natal."

"It was nothing," he said. "I could fight or I could die. I chose not to die. But it will impress the voters, who have always been more concerned with bravery than accomplishment."

"Winning these medals was a major accomplishment," I corrected him. "A splendid one."

"Well," he said, "let us hope the public is as easily beguiled by them as you are."

"These three," I said, indicating the three medals for Outstanding Bravery. "What particular actions were they for?"

"This one," he said, "was for attacking the enemy's flagship while in a small shuttlecraft." He snorted contemptuously. "As if I had a choice. The shuttle was three thousand miles away from the mother ship when the enemy suddenly appeared between us."

"And the other two?"

He shrugged. "I've no idea. You would have to ask the man I took them from."

"You *stole* them?" I asked.

"Only after he attacked me in a drunken rage and I killed him. If he was brave enough to win them, and I was brave enough to defend myself and take them away from him, then I won them by proxy." A quick smile. "And I will make sure no one asks me about their origin during the campaign."

"You have only one month before the election," I noted. "Perhaps it will not come up." Then: "When will you go to Ulundi to begin campaigning?"

"As soon as you take me there," he replied.

"I can't," I said. "I told you—I have a job and responsibilities."

"Forget them," he said. "You are working for me now."

"I am?" I said with a smile. "When is payday?"

"Soon," he said with no show of embarrassment.

"Soon," I repeated sardonically.

"And often."

I knew I should refuse, that I should put him on public transport to Ulundi the next morning and show up at my job, as boring and poorly paid as it was, but I must confess that I was curious to watch him campaign—he always had such control of his emotions that I wanted to see how he whipped a crowd into a frenzy while remaining cool and collected himself. Then, too, if he was successful, if he actually gained a modicum of political power, there was the possibility that I could do more good for more people than just teaching one impoverished group of children. I would miss them, and I hoped they would miss me, but if things worked out maybe I could help them more in Ulundi than in the classroom.

I called in sick, we arrived in Ulundi the next afternoon, Robert registered his party and announced his candidacy, and then we took a room in a hotel that was one step above being a flophouse.

The next morning Hector ole Kunene failed to show up at a small breakfast for the party faithful. He didn't appear for a noon interview and an afternoon rally, and in fact was never seen again.

And twenty-seven days later Robert ole Buthelezi, representing the Zulu Party, won an uncontested election for the office of Clerk of Records.

It didn't seem like much at the time, but years later historians would want all the details, however insignificant.

4.

WHEN ROBERT TOOK OFFICE, HE gave me an imposing title—Vice Chairman and Confidential Advisor—but I was just a glorified filing clerk. I suppose I should have quit after the first week and gone back home, but my paycheck after that week was more than I made in a month as a teacher. I couldn't figure it out—I was clearly a flunky, nothing more—but somehow when Robert put through the voucher for my salary, no one argued with him. Which was probably just as well; Robert did not lose very many arguments. I sent half of my check to the school, and decided to stay.

Ulundi wasn't Johannesburg or Pretoria, but it was still far more sophisticated than the town where I had been living. A monorail circled the city, two matching skyscrapers reached for the clouds, and the city's power was now supplied by nuclear energy.

Each evening I stopped by a local restaurant on my way back to my rented room. From time to time Robert would choose to eat there, but never alone. Invariably he was in the company of men I did not know. Some were very well dressed, and often had their government ID tags still affixed to their tunics. Others were poorly dressed, and made no attempt to hide the fact that they carried weapons. It made no difference to Robert; he was equally at home with all of them.

Well, perhaps I should reword that: he was equally comfortable and self-contained with either group. I don't know for a fact that I ever saw him actually *enjoy* another man's company. I know that he enjoyed the company of women, but not in that way and not in public.

We had been in Ulundi for about four months when he finally invited me out to dinner. It was the first meal we had eaten together since we had arrived in the city. He took me to a posh restaurant, where all the staff seemed to know him (as did many of the diners), and we were escorted to a table in the farthest corner of the room.

"This is my regular table here," he said as we sat down. "I do not believe any other diners can overhear me here as long as I keep my voice down."

"I would think they have very little interest in governmental recordkeeping anyway," I said.

He laughed, the first laugh I had heard him utter since he returned after his ten-year absence.

"If there was any doubt that we are brothers, that eradicates it," he said. "Our father had a sense of humor too—or so I have been told." Neither of us remembered much of Buthelezi, who had wandered off one day and never returned. In truth, we had no idea if he was still alive.

"I am sure it will be a very fine meal," I said, "and I will speak so softly no one can possibly overhear me, but I still don't know why I am here."

"To make plans, of course."

"Just me?" I asked. I stared at him curiously. "Am I being fired?"

"No, and no," he said. "But if we are to move to Pretoria in a few months, we must prepare."

"*Are* we moving to Pretoria?"

He nodded his head. "I told you we would not be in Ulundi for long."

"You have found a better job?" I asked.

"I have served my apprenticeship," he answered. "It is time to become President."

"Based on three medals, two of which aren't yours, and four months as Clerk of Records in a backwater province?" I said.

"It *is* a backwater province," he replied. "It is time to leave it."

"I have no problem with that," I said. "But to think you can become the President of all South Africa…"

"It is the logical next step in the progression."

"The progression?" I said, surprised. "You mean there's more?"

He looked at me rather sadly, the way you might look at a pet that will never understand what you are trying to teach it.

"There is more."

"The Presidency of South Africa"—an impossibility in itself—"isn't enough?"

"When Tchaka became king of the Zulus, Zululand was perhaps ten square miles," he shot back. "Was *that* enough?"

"He controlled only ten square miles; the President controls hundreds of thousands," I said. "There's a difference."

"Only in degree," replied Robert. "*His* world covered the southern tip of Africa. *Mine* extends as far as the eye can see."

"So did his," I argued.

Robert gave me another sad smile reserved for pets of limited intelligence. "He never looked *up*."

5.

Lloyds of London had the odds against him at 200-to-1 with eleven weeks to go. The one casino in Las Vegas that booked bets on it lowered it to 175-to-1 in case there was a sympathy vote for the poor clerk who had the temerity to buck the entrenched political machine. Robert borrowed a thousand rands and bet on himself.

Two months before the election, there was a debate between the three leading candidates. Well, actually, the two leading candidates and Robert. It was held in a stadium in Cape Town, rather than a holo studio, and some forty thousand people were in attendance. It was a bright, sunlit day, as almost all days on the Cape are, and it was estimated that more than eighty million people, in South Africa and elsewhere, were watching on their Tri Ds and their computers' holoscreens.

They were about half an hour into the debate when it happened. Three gunmen—one armed with a laser gun, two with projectile pistols—burst onto the floor of the stadium. They must have been hiding in the laundry facilities in the back of the visiting team's clubhouse, and had killed half a dozen security men along the way. They raced onto the field where one of the network anchors was acting as moderator for the debate. One of them started yelling something—the sound system couldn't pick it up—and then they began firing their weapons. The guards were taken by surprise, and soon lay dead on the stadium floor.

One man fired a shot at Robert, who threw himself to the ground. The bullet hit a woman in the stands. She screamed and pitched forward, dead.

The President was crouching down behind his podium, and the man with the laser pistol was burning his way through it. Two shots tore into the other candidate, blood spurted out of his throat, and he collapsed, writhing and twisting frantically for a few seconds, then lay absolutely still in an ever-increasing pool of his own blood.

And then, just as everyone thought there was more slaughter to come, Robert got to his feet and raced to the man with the laser, hurtling himself against the man's back and sending him sprawling. Somehow he got his hand on the gun as the two went down in a heap and he came up firing. The first blast of deadly light turned one of the pistols to molten metal, the second went right between the third man's eyes. The man whose gun had melted threw himself at Robert, which was all but suicidal: I don't think Robert had ever lost a fight since he began building his body up after that one experience as a boy. He reached out a long, powerful arm, grabbed the man by the throat, lifted him off the ground until the wild thrashing became feeble twitching, and then literally threw him away.

The first gunman, the one with the laser who he had disarmed, got up, took one look into Robert's eyes, didn't like what he saw, spotted some police running onto the field, and raced to them, his arms in the air, screaming that he surrendered.

Robert walked over to where the President cowered behind the podium, gently lifted him to his feet, and kept a steadying arm around him until the medics arrived about a minute later.

It was not only an act of extreme heroism, but it had been seen by eighty million people, two-thirds of them eligible to vote in the upcoming election. That night Lloyds lowered his odds to four-to-one, and within a week, when matched against the President, it was six-to-five pick 'em. By Election

Day, Robert was an odds-on favorite, and he won the way a heavy favorite should.

The morning after the election, he issued executive pardons to the two surviving would-be assassins. There was some brief outrage in the press, but he pointed out that if he, who had literally risked his life to prevent them from killing the President, was willing to forgive them, what right did anyone else have to hold a grudge?

"That was a remarkable act of generosity," I remarked when he and I were briefly alone in his office. I had been appointed his Chief of Staff, but it was entirely for show; he saw who he wanted, when he wanted.

"You have no idea," he replied with an unfathomable smile.

"I think the people will love you all the more for it: a hero—but a hero with compassion."

"The thought had crossed my mind," he said dryly.

"I can't get over how serendipitous it was," I continued. "I think you were actually winning the debate, and it probably wouldn't have won you ten extra votes. But those crazed killers showed up and suddenly you're the biggest hero we've had since…well, Nelson Mandala was a Xhosa, so…since Shaka himself."

"His name, as I keep telling you, was Tchaka," replied Robert. "And the most serendipitous thing in the past month is that Lloyds paid off promptly."

"I didn't know you needed money."

He shrugged. "If I hadn't been elected, I wouldn't have needed it."

"I don't understand," I said.

"You will," he replied. "The day after tomorrow Dlamini and Gumbi"—the two surviving assassins—"will be released. We'll give the press a few days to ask them the usual endlessly stupid questions. Then, by next week, when the interest and the crowd have died down, you'll pay them a visit."

"And?"

"And give each of them half of my Lloyds winnings."

"You hired them?" I said, wondering why I didn't feel more shocked at the revelation.

"Be a realist, John," he answered easily. "What killer in his right mind commits murder—or tries to—in front of eighty million viewers?"

I stared at him for a long moment. "Welcome to the wonderful world of politics," I said bitterly.

He shook his head. "No, John," he corrected me. "Welcome to winning."

6.

I was Robert's appointment—the Postmaster for all South Africa. I have to admit that he was an exceptionally effective President for the first year. The unions had a stranglehold on labor. He broke it. Not with armies of thugs as unions had been fought in the past, but with the carrot and the stick.

Every government agency, from the spaceport traffic controllers to the servants in the Parliament's private dining room, was run with union labor. He went out of his way to antagonize the unions, and every time a union struck, he would fire all the members who were working for the government, declaring that that particular union or brotherhood of unions could no longer expect government contracts in the future. Then, a week later, he offered work to the same employees who had been fired, usually at twenty percent more than they had been making—and that came to even more money when they realized they did not have to pay union dues.

When the mine owners began to speak about running a candidate to oppose him in the next election, he nationalized the biggest mining company, and the rest of the owners took the hint.

Namibia, to the west of us, opposed a trade policy. He cut off all trade until they decided the policy wasn't so bad after all.

He was a masterful politician, adept at all forms of power politics. In less than two years he had the shining, modern capital of South Africa—and indeed the whole country—running like clockwork. Not all the people were happy, not all the businesses were prospering, but he had enough of both on his side that he had nothing to worry about. I thought this would give him an incentive to relax and slow down, but it seemed to have just the opposite effect.

For two years he had a map of South Africa on the wall to the left of his desk. Then one day it was gone, and was replaced by a map of the lower half of the African continent. That afternoon I was summoned to his office.

"Yes, Mr. President?" I said, for I always referred to him by his formal title.

"John, my brother," he said, "I think your talents are being wasted. You are my Postmaster, and yet hardly anyone uses the post office any more. It's been decades since anyone sent a letter, even a legal document, by mail rather than electronically, and as for parcels, we are competing with half a dozen carriers. Our postal service is an anachronism; I foresee better things for you."

I remained silent, trying to figure out what he was leading up to, since we had never discussed my future, only his, and only in grandiose if non-specific terms.

"As of this afternoon, you are my ambassador to Mozambique."

"Mozambique?" I repeated, surprised. It was an impoverished neighboring country, and our primary interaction with them was turning back thousands of illegal immigrants at the border every day.

He nodded. "Don't look so disappointed. This is a very important posting."

"Perhaps you will explain what makes it so?" I said, for in my mind it was actually a lesser position than Postmaster, which wasn't much to begin with.

He smiled. "Take a week to find your way around Beira. Play some golf, visit the casino, do a little sailing."

"It sounds easy enough," I said, waiting for the other shoe to drop.

"At the end of the week, you will pay a visit to the President of Mozambique and deliver *this*." He handed me an envelope bearing the official seal of the President. Another smile. "It will be your last duty as Postmaster."

"What's in it?"

"Our demand that they turn over their half of the Krueger National Park to us. It was unfairly divided centuries ago."

"Do we care?" I asked. "Are you planning on building a city on park land?"

"Certainly not. It is home to the last wild animals on the continent. I wouldn't dream of changing it."

"Then I repeat—what is this all about?"

"We want restitution for all the centuries that they have profited from land that should legally have been ours," said Robert.

"What are you talking about?" I said. "The land was divided by a treaty that was ratified and signed by both countries."

He shook his head. "It was signed by white squatters who took the land and the government away from the indigent peoples. It is not a legal treaty."

"Mozambique has no money," I persisted. "What can they be making in park fees? Three thousand rands a year, if that?"

"I know. That is why we will not ask for money."

"I thought you said you wanted restitution."

"I do," he replied.

"I don't understand."

He walked to the map and pulled a pen out of his pocket. "This is approximate," he said, drawing a line across the lower third of Mozambique. "*This* will constitute our restitution."

I stared at the map in silence for a moment. "You can't be serious," I said, although I knew he was.

"It is prime pastureland," replied Robert. "There are rivers than can be diverted to South Africa during droughts. There is a huge population that has been trying to cross our border for generations, and will be happy to work for whatever wages we offer them, however minimal—and that in turn will keep our own people in line."

"Mozambique will never agree to it," I said.

"And we have a well-trained army," he continued, "an army that needs something to do."

"It'll be a slaughter."

"It will be a good training exercise.""

"You sound like there's more," I said.

"We have treaties with Namibia, Botswana, Zimbabwe, Angola…"

"Just how far north to you plan to go?" I demanded.

"Have you ever seen the Mediterranean, my brother?" he asked. "It is quite beautiful this time of year."

"There have been wars of conquest on this continent before."

"Led by madmen and fools," he replied. "I am neither."

"You really mean to do it?"

He gestured toward the letter. "It is done."

"Then let someone else deliver it," I said. "I'll stay where I am."

"My mind is made up," he said. "You will be my ambassador to Mozambique."

"Why me?" I asked. "You have generals and hirelings who would love to make the President of Mozambique squirm."

"That is precisely why I want you," said Robert. "You are a compassionate man who will sympathize with him." He shot me a triumphant smile. "I know you give most of your salary to local orphanages. You even feet stray dogs and cats. You cannot hide your nature from me, my brother, and you will not be able to hide it from him."

"What has that to do with anything?"

"When you tell him, truthfully and in some detail, exactly what will befall him and his people should he refuse my demands, when he sees that you actually *care*, that you do not want his country to become a smoking junk-heap, he will know that I mean what I say, and further, he will know precisely because of your reaction, that I have to power to do what I say."

"Am I then to become your ambassador to every other country you wish to conquer?" I asked bitterly.

"I have no interest in conquest," he said.

"Oh? What *do* you call it?"

"Assimilation," he replied. "We are one land mass. Once, there were twenty-three hundred tribes, twenty-three hundred separate nation-states, living on this continent. Then the Europeans gave us false borders, and suddenly there were fifty-one countries. It is time for one more redrawing of the map: one continent, one country."

"And one ruler?" I asked.

"And one ruler," he agreed.

I delivered the envelope to the President of Mozambique exactly one week later. He opened it, read it, frowned, and asked me if the President was serious, or if this was a bad joke. I assured him that Robert ole Buthelezi was in deadly earnest, and urged him to relinquish the land rather than enter a war he couldn't possibly win.

He was a proud man, and he tore the demand up, put it back in the envelope, and told me to deliver it to the President.

Three weeks later the South African third, fifth and eighth divisions marched across the Krueger Park and into Mozambique. The Mozambique army fought bravely, but they were outnumbered, outgunned, and overmatched. Within ten days every one of them was dead or a prisoner of war, and Robert announced to his people that South Africa's territory had just increased by more than sixty thousand square miles.

It would not be the last such announcement that he would make.

7.

FIVE MONTHS LATER, WHEN ROBERT threatened to go to war with Namibia over water rights, they surrendered without a shot being fired. He politely suggested that they might like to become a protectorate, or better still, a province, and they agreed.

Botswana saw what was happening, and they knew that they were the treasure of Southern Africa because they sat on the largest diamond pipes, larger and more productive than South Africa in its heyday. They were the only African nation besides our own that could truly be said to have a thriving economy.

And they knew how to use that economy. I was in the Presidential Palace when the first word came through: our crack sixth division had been turned back at the Botswana border, with better than fifty percent casualties.

We knew it couldn't be the Botswana army, because Botswana didn't *have* an army. It was eighty percent Kalahari Desert, and another ten percent Okavango Swamp. Even in the twenty-fifth century, the population hadn't reached three million. Almost all of them lived along the Limpopo River, and they had not gone to war with anyone in their entire history.

It didn't take long to find out what had happened. The rest of the continent—indeed, the world—was not unaware of what was happening down at the southern tip of Africa, and Botswana had used some of its wealth to hire an army of mercenaries, led by an American veteran of the Battle of Io, a Colonel McBride. They had the latest weapons, the latest technology, and an employer that was willing to supply them with whatever they needed to preserve its territorial integrity.

Robert, who usually dined at the finest restaurants in Pretoria, chose to have dinner in his expansive office. He invited three of us—two political advisors, whose advice he never listened to, and myself—to join him in the huge, carpeted room that was dominated by two paintings of Robert himself, one staring down at his desk, the other looking out over the balcony at the extensive, exquisitely manicured grounds.

"You look troubled," I said when I entered the office, the last to arrive.

"They are fucking up my timetable!" he growled.

"Perhaps we should just leave them be," said an advisor. "After all, they are a useful trading partner."

"And back down in the eyes of the world?" snapped Robert. "Never!" He turned to me. "You are my brother. My blood runs in your veins. What would *you* do?"

I stared at him blankly. "Send more troops?" I said at last.

"Then they will buy more mercenaries, and our soldiers will kill their mercenaries and their mercenaries will kill our soldiers. We will win in the long run, because our population is larger than their diamond mines, but I do not want Botswana if it is impoverished and destroyed by the war. So what would you do?"

I shrugged. "I don't know what you want me to say."

"Blood may be thicker than water," he said contemptuously. "It is clearly not more intelligent." He looked around the room. "Can no one else see the way?"

Silence.

"I wonder why I pay you at all," he muttered.

The food arrived and we moved to an imported mahogany table that four soldiers carried into the office and set up for us.

"Let me do the honors," said Robert. He took a pitcher of cold water in his hand, and we passed him our glasses. A tiny smile played around the corners of his mouth, and he slowly poured the contents of the pitcher onto the plush carpet. "*Now* does anyone see the way?"

We were all silent.

"Fools!" he snapped. "Botswana is a desert. It is fed only by three rivers—the Limpopo, the Okavango, and the Chobe. The Okavango and the Chobe originate in Namibia, which we now own, and the Limpopo originates very near Pretoria and flows into it from South Africa."

"You are going to cut off their water?" asked an advisor.

"We will begin diverting or damming all three rivers tomorrow. They cannot mine for diamonds without massive amounts of water. Given a choice, they will save the water for their people. Hopefully the mercenaries will see that their source of income is literally drying up, and will go where the money is and fight in some other war."

"And if not?"

"If not, they will be so weakened from thirst by the time we confront them again that they will prove very easy to subdue."

"How long will you wait?" I asked.

"As long as it takes. At least a year. The Okavango Delta will not dry up before then. And we'll see if the government wants to keep paying a mercenary army when it is not under attack."

"And the tens of thousands of women and children who will die of thirst?" I asked angrily.

"They would have died of *something* sooner or later," he said with no show of concern. "And those who do not die will be so thrilled to have the rivers unblocked again that they will strew flowers in our path."

I thought it was cruel beyond belief. These weren't soldiers or mercenaries we were talking about, but citizens who he would coldly condemn to a terrible death. The problem was that I couldn't see any way it could fail.

Within a week work had begun on all three rivers, and within two months they had been dammed or diverted. Robert was prepared to wait two years, perhaps three, to bring Botswana to its knees—

—but Botswana wasn't willing to wait. They had a mercenary army, they couldn't afford to keep them (or supply them with water) indefinitely, and they decided not to wait. News of the first incursion over our northern border reached us on a Sunday. By Tuesday, before Robert could mobilize our near-dormant air force, Colonel McBride's men had progressed as far as Pilanesburg, and citizens in both the political capital of Pretoria and the economic capital of Johannesburg were getting nervous.

Three members of the Parliament called for Robert's resignation. They did not show up the next day, or ever again, but there was still serious unrest in the government.

It began to look like McBride might reach Pretoria in another seven to ten days. Then a small private plane crashed very near the main body of McBride's troops, and within a day almost seventy percent of them were dead.

"What the hell happened?" asked an advisor when Robert summoned us to tell us that the war was as good as over and that we had won.

"If I were to guess," said Robert, "I would guess that a plane loaded with a particularly virulent form of mutated visceral leishmaniasis lost control and crashed within the middle of Colonel McBride's forces."

"Are you crazy?" demanded the advisor. "Germ warfare has been outlawed for centuries!"

"I was defending my country," said Robert calmly. "How will the Western nations, with whom I have signed no agreement or treaty, punish us—by sending bigger germs?"

"But this will kill our own people too!"

"They are not our people," replied Robert. "They are Xhosa and Mtebele. We are Zulu."

"They are South Africans, and you are their President!"

"Then they will have died for their country, and their families will honor their memories."

"I just want it on record that I strongly disapprove," said the advisor.

Robert shrugged. "You have that right."

The advisor left the room. No one ever saw him again.

Soon the reports began coming in. Nothing was alive within twenty-five miles of the crash—and ninety percent of McBride's forces had been that close to it. None of the local residents had survived either.

A few stray mercenaries, far out on the flanks, or advance scouts, were alive but grievously ill. Robert refused to allow them access to our medical facilities, and they were airlifted to Gaborone, where I am told most of them died within a week.

"It's just as well," said Robert a few days later. "It could have taken as much as three years to starve them out. This saved a lot of time and effort."

"But not lives," I noted bitterly.

"I'm alive," he shot back. "You're alive. We have a new province almost the size of Spain, and almost none of the population died in the conflict. What more could you want?"

I couldn't think of any response that would alter his perceptions, so I remained silent.

"Anyway," he continued, "since McBride is dead and there is no one left of any rank to surrender to me here, I suppose I shall have to fly to Gaborone and allow them to surrender to me there."

"Don't we have an ambassador there?" I asked.

"Presidents do not surrender to ambassadors or underlings," said Robert. "I will go myself."

And so he did. But first he got our finest calligrapher to draw up a list of his demands, and write them in beautiful script on an actual piece of parchment. Then, armed with that, he traveled to Gaborone, accompanied only by me, an advisor, and a small handful of bodyguards.

A huge crowd gathered as he climbed the steps of the Presidential mansion. The Botswanan President, a withered, elderly man who looked like he hadn't slept in a week, greeted him at the top of the stairs, and the two of them went into his office. They emerged half an hour later, and Robert walked through the ornate entry hall to the top of the steps, holding the signed parchment aloft.

"Citizens!" he cried. "I bring glad tidings! Beginning this week, the rivers shall flow again." A huge cheer. "Beginning this week, you will never have to rely on a hired military that owes no allegiance to you, for you will be protected against all external threats by the army of South Africa." Another cheer. "And beginning right now you will never again be led by a weakling such as this man standing next to me." And before anyone realized what was happening, Robert had pulled a pistol out of his pocket, placed it against the President's head, and pulled the trigger.

The explosion brought a shocked gasp from the crowd, as the withered man collapsed in a heap. I thought they were going to race up the stairs and attack Robert, but he held up a hand. It didn't mean anything, but it was a dramatic gesture, and it got their attention.

"All he brought you was thirst and defeat. Now things will be different. To begin with, I am declaring a two-week paid holiday for every worker in Botswana. And if any employer doesn't honor that promise," he added sternly, "I want to know about it." I saw the members of the crowd looking at each other, puzzled expressions on their faces. "Furthermore, to welcome you into the nation of South Africa, I am also declaring a one-year moratorium on all taxes."

This time a cheer arose, and Robert shot me a "Did you really think they'd attack me?" smile.

"Finally," he continued, "all political prisoners will be freed tomorrow morning, and their prison records expunged."

I wasn't aware of any political prisoners in Botswana, and I was sure Robert wasn't either, but it brought an exuberant round of applause, and I could see the faces in crowd, each seeming to say, "This isn't the disaster we'd feared," and then, "This was a blessing in disguise!"

A woman suddenly shouted out: "Hallelujah!"

Then a gravel-voiced man climbed the first couple of stairs, turned to his compatriots, and yelled, "Three cheers for Buthelezi!"

The crowd was about to accommodate him when Robert held up his hand again.

"Thank you," he said, stepping over the dead body of the President and walking a few steps closer to them, "but Buthelezi was an insignificant flyspeck on the dungheap of humanity. I reject that name."

"What shall we call you then?" asked another man.

He drew himself up to his full height and looked out at the crowd.

"Tchaka," he answered.

8.

I THOUGHT WHEN WORD GOT out the people would be outraged. After all, Shaka was the father of the Zulu people, the reason we ruled the world—well, *our* world—for almost a century, the reason even men in the farthest reaches of Europe, Asia and America knew that the Zulus were the fiercest, mightiest warriors. And here was my brother, not much over thirty, of obscure birth, a stranger to morality, taking that name for himself.

And to my surprise, the citizens were thrilled beyond belief—and when I looked at it from their point of view, it suddenly made sense. He was the first Zulu to preside over South Africa since our humiliating defeats just before the turn of the twentieth century. He had doubled our land with the addition of Mozambique, Nambia and Botswana. Other African nations were racing to form alliances with the Europeans and Americans, with the Chinese and Indians and Australians, all because they knew that this Zulu leader would soon be looking north. It was the second coming of Shaka, and their joy and pride knew no bounds.

Something else that knew no bounds was my brother's ambition.

His first step was to dissolve the Parliament. None of our African neighbors said a word—they were too busy preparing to defend their borders—but the rest of the world reacted with outrage. They demanded that Parliament be restored. Tchaka responded by announcing that he was resigning from the Presidency. The world breathed a sigh of relief. It lasted three days—until his coronation as king.

"They will never stand for this," I said when the ceremony was over. We were in his office, and he had removed the ceremonial crown and robes and sat at his desk, relaxed in a tunic and slacks.

"Of course they will," he replied easily. "If they stood for my annexing Botswana and Mozambique, they will stand for my wearing a crown, for nothing else has changed."

"You have gone too far," I said.

"I have barely begun," he replied, and suddenly I knew that when he looked to the north, he looked beyond Zimbabwe, beyond the Congo, beyond Egypt, that he looked north to Polaris and the stars beyond it. "They are civilized men," he said, his face contorting in a sneer at the word, "and they will behave in a civilized manner. They will talk, and talk some more, and threaten, and entreat, and eventually they will bribe, and finally they will shrug and learn to live with the situation. Mark my words: you will never see a single European or American or Asian soldier enter our land with hostile intent."

And somehow I knew he was right.

The international cries of outrage began that night. Every newsdisk, every holo, every diplomatic missive demanded that he resign and restore the constitution. He ignored them all for almost a month, and when the rest of the world had whipped itself into a frenzy, he announced that he would address the world via a holo transmission that would be seen on every continent.

The so-called Great Powers thought they had won, that he was preparing to make a resignation speech and, in essence, make peace with the rest of the world, but those of us who knew him best knew better. I got the distinct feeling that he was toying with them the way a cat toys with a mouse, that far from feeling any pressure he was enjoying their discomfiture enormously.

Finally the night came. I had expected him to wear a conservative suit, or even a tuxedo, but instead he wore a tattered tribal robe and a tarnished, unimpressive replica of his crown.

"It will put them at their ease," he said with a smile. "After all, they think they are dealing with a barbarian. I wouldn't want to disappoint them by not looking the part."

An aide brought him an iced tea, and he began sipping it calmly.

"You are about to address fourteen billion people," I said. "Aren't you at all nervous?"

"It is *they* who should be nervous, not I," he replied.

Soon the time arrived, and the rest of us moved out of camera range while he seated himself behind his desk, waited for the half-dozen cameras to position themselves, and then nodded to the director, whose sole duty seemed to be to count down and tell the cameramen when to start shooting.

"Good evening," he said in perfect English. "I am speaking to you because some grievous wrongs have been done, and I have been asked to put them right again. This I shall do to the best of my ability."

There was a screen in the corner of the room, showing the reaction of the huge crowd just outside the Presidential Palace, and I could see them mouthing the words: "No, Tchaka! No!" But there was no sound in the office, other than my brother's voice.

"I think everyone listening will agree that it is immoral, indeed evil, to take another people's land by force—and this is something I would never do." He held up three treaties. "These are treaties I have signed with the leaders of the former nations of Namibia, Mozambique and Botswana, in which they petitioned me to annex their countries into the Union of South Africa, and since that was the wish of their people, I acceded to their request."

He paused and looked at the camera. "South Africa did not take their land by force, but at their own request. Any other reason would have been against the laws of God and man. Therefore, I must—in keeping with my earlier pledge to you—demand that the United States of America forthwith return its entire holdings on the North American continent to the Native Americans from whom they stole it. By the same token, I demand that the British give up all claim to…" He ran through a list of most of the Commonwealth countries, then did the same for the French and the Russians.

"I cannot, of course, force these nations to do the right thing, but I will lend my support to those who oppose their policies."

He stared unblinking at the camera. "Next, I want to address the question of hereditary royalty. I should begin by saying that I am not king because my father was. There is no royal blood in my veins. Indeed, there is no royal blood in the whole of South Africa. I became king by the will of my people, and should I produce a son, he will have no more claim on that title than any other South African. We believe that a throne must be *earned*, not given."

A pause, and then a frown. "In keeping with that philosophy, I urge the monarchs of England, the Netherlands, Jordan, Syria,"—he named another dozen countries—"all monarchs solely by the accident of birth, to relinquish their thrones forthwith."

I glanced at the screen showing the street again. The people were cheering so hard that I was surprised we couldn't feel the vibrations here in the building.

"I hope that by explaining my positions I have eliminated any misunderstandings," he concluded. "There have been many lies told about me, and many lies of a different sort told about the people who rule you. Now I have spoken, and I leave it to you, the people of the world, to determine the truth of things."

The director indicated that the transmission was over, and Tchaka stood up and thanked all the technicians for their efforts. They filed out of the office, taking their equipment with them, and he sent for another iced tea.

"Those lights are hot," he said, mopping the sweat from his forehead.

"You were brilliant tonight," said an aide. "Now the rest of the world will leave us alone."

"Do you really think so?" asked Tchaka.

"Of course."

"You're fired." The aide looked stunned. "There are enough fools abroad in the land," continued Tchaka. "I do not need any on my staff." He turned to me. "What will the world do, my brother?"

"They will say that you are an evil twister of words, a madman with designs on the entire continent, a villain not to be trusted." Suddenly I could not repress a smile. "But I think they will not discuss royalty again."

He smiled back at me. "They will say all of that," he agreed. "And they will be wrong."

"That you are not a villain or that you are not a madman?" I asked.

"That I have designs on the African continent," he replied.

"Don't you?"

He smiled. It was an almost terrifying smile. "If you were hungry and you found yourself in an orchard, would you settle for only one piece of fruit off a tree?"

"The *world*?" asked an advisor, surprised by my brother's audacity.

Tchaka shook his head. "You still do not understand."

The man looked at him with a blank expression.

Tchaka walked to a window and pulled back the curtain. "The world is just one tree." He waved his hand at the heavens. "I shall have an orchard."

9.

THE HISTORICAL SHAKA HAD A witch doctor whose counsel he trusted. My brother had an astrologer. His name was William James Hlatshwayo, and he had earned his Master of Science degree from the University of California. I preferred to think of it as a Master of Pseudoscience degree, but Tchaka conferred with him daily and waited patiently, not while he rolled the bones, but rather while he read the stars and cast his horoscopes.

I don't know where my brother found him, or when. All I know is that one day he showed up, and from that day forth he had more influence on Tchaka than any other man alive.

I argued against him. I pointed out that Tchaka had won the Presidency without an *umthagkathi*—a word I uttered with contempt, for it is the Zulu word for witch doctor—and had annexed three countries without him, and had become king without him, so why listen to him now?

"Because up to this point, my brother," Tchaka answered me, "I have been only a caterpillar. A successful one, to be sure, but a caterpillar. Soon, though, I shall break out of my chrysalis and spread my wings. There will be no limit to the heights to which I can soar."

"But—" I began, but he held up a hand for silence.

"Even the butterfly has predators, and the higher he flies, the less they are known to him. If William can warn me of some enemies of which I am not aware, then I would be a fool not to make use of him."

"And if he is a fraud?"

"Then I am no greater danger than I was before."

"You would be better off with a true *umthagkathi*," I said, "for this man's science is no science at all."

"You know nothing about it," said Tchaka placidly.

"I know this," I said. "The science of astrology is based on the calendar, is it not?"

"Yes."

"And it is three thousand years old?"

"Older," said Tchaka.

"There you have it," I said.

"There I have *what*?" he asked irritably.

"Astrology is based on the calendar, and it uses the calendar, is that correct?"

"You know that."

"Then explain this," I said triumphantly. "The science was created more than three thousand years ago, yet Julius Caesar and Augustus Caesar lived less than twenty-five hundred years ago. The months of July and August are named for them, and did not exist when astrology was created, so how true a science can it be?"

"Doubtless the names were substituted for other names," he replied. "That has nothing to do with science, only with nomenclature."

"*Astrology* has nothing to do with science," I persisted. "If you let yourself be guided by him long enough, eventually your *umthagkathi* will get us all killed."

"I am Tchaka," he said, as if the words were identical to "I cannot die."

"Fine," I said. "You are immortal. Your army is not, and your government is not. What good is your immortality if all around you have died because some arrant fraud tells you to do something because the moon is here or Mars is there?"

He was silent for a long moment, and finally he spoke. "I have listened patiently to you, my brother. I have heard your words and considered them." His expression hardened. "And I have rejected them. We will not speak of this again, and you will never call him an *umthagkathi* in my presence. Is that understand?"

I looked into his eyes, which were the doorway to his soul, and as usual there was no softness, no give whatsoever.

"It is understood," I replied.

"Good," he said. "Because great deeds lay ahead of us. *Great* deeds." He paused. "Tomorrow I will meet with a representative from America."

"A new ambassador?" I suggested. It was common knowledge that most of the countries of the world had withdrawn their ambassadors and closed their embassies after Tchaka's speech, but that had been a few months earlier and it was time for them to rethink their positions, as Western governments always did.

"No, a businessman," said Tchaka.

"Well, at least America has lifted the ban on its citizens visiting us."

"No, it hasn't," said Tchaka in amused tones. "But I have something they want, so they are assiduously looking the other way, and will someday claim that they had no knowledge of this visit or its outcome."

"And what is the nature of this visit?" I asked.

"Two weeks ago I sold a fifty-year lease on the two largest diamond pipes in Botswana to the Chinese," he began. "I then leased all the other diamond concessions to England and Brazil."

"You sold the entire wealth of a nation?" I said, startled. "Why?"

"Leased, not sold," he corrected me. "And the reason I did is because I needed the money for tomorrow's dealings with our American visitor."

"Whatever he's selling, it must be very expensive, if it's worth a half-century supply of diamonds from the most diamond-rich country in the world," I said.

"Oh, it is," he replied with a smile. "*Very* expensive. Plundering Botswana's riches for only a quarter or a third of a century would not have been sufficient."

I just stared at him, wondering what could possibly cost as much as he seemed willing to pay.

"Well," he said, clearly enjoying my confusion, "aren't you going to ask?"

"What are you buying from the American?" I said.

He reached into a desk drawer and pulled out a shining model of the latest starfaring military ship, much advanced over the type he'd served on less than a decade ago.

"You've bought a starship?" I asked incredulously.

He chuckled in amusement. "For plundering an entire country for half a century? I am a better bargainer than that, my brother." He paused. "The American is here today, but Hlatshwayo tells me the stars are not yet in the proper alignment. Tomorrow I will meet with him and finalize the purchase of an entire fleet of starships," he concluded proudly.

"And what of Botswana?" I asked.

"It has been here for a thousand centuries or more," he replied. "It has lived its life. It is the past." He pointed a forefinger toward the ceiling, and beyond that, the sky. "The future is out there—a million worlds for the taking."

"And if someone objects to your just going out and taking them?" I asked.

"That is their choice," he said with no show of concern. "Mine has already been made."

At that instant I didn't know who I felt sorrier for—Botswana or the galaxy.

10.

As Tchaka was building his fleet, two of our colonies—one on Delta Pavonis, one on Cygni 2—came under attack. For weeks we didn't know who was responsible for it. Then our experts discovered that they were a previously-unknown race from DX Cancri.

Earth mobilized and soon assembled a fleet of some three thousand ships under the leadership of the brilliant American commander, Delores Sanchez—and Tchaka announced that South Africa would join the fleet with an independent force of our own.

Word came back quickly. The military thanked Tchaka for his offer, but all ships would be under the command of Admiral Sanchez.

Tchaka's response was direct and to the point:

I take orders from no one. Do you want us to fight your enemy or don't you?

From Planetary Command:

These are your enemies too.

And from Tchaka:

They have not harmed South Africa or any of its possessions. We are an independent nation, beholden to no one, and we choose our own enemies. If you want our help, you know our terms.

There was no official reply.

"They want us," said Tchaka. "They just don't want to admit it."

"How can you be so sure?" I asked.

"Because if they didn't need us, they would reject my offer without hesitation." He smiled. "It is good to know our enemy's weaknesses."

"Our enemy is out there," I said, pointing to the stars.

He sighed and shook his head sadly. "You are so slow to learn, my brother."

"Learn what?"

"They are *all* our enemies," he replied.

"How can you say that?" I said.

"They are not Zulus," he answered, as if that explained it all.

Over the next month we began testing our new ships and recruiting a navy for them. We received no official communication from Earth's united military command, but word reached us through unofficial channels that when we were ready, they would prefer us to concentrate on Delta Pavonis.

"Of course they would," said Tchaka with a sardonic smile.

"Why do you say it like that?" asked an aide.

"It's almost twice as far from Earth as Cygni 2," he replied. "It will require twice as much fuel, if we run into trouble it will take reinforcements twice as long to come to our aid, and for all we know the main body of the enemy fleet is there. When they evaluate their forces, you may be sure that we are the most expendable."

"So do we accommodate the military, or do we go to Cygni-2?" asked another aide.

"In either location there will be hundreds, perhaps thousands, of ships from Earth. I have no intention of being a cog in their war machine." He paused. "Every army and navy must have a supply line. We'll patrol the least likely route between DX Cancri and Delta Pavonis."

"The *least* likely?" asked the aide, frowning in puzzlement.

"If *I* know the enemy requires supplies, don't you think Commander Sanchez knows it too, and will patrol all the likely shipping lanes between the planets?"

"If we choose the wrong route, will she think we are trying to avoid the battle?"

Tchaka stared at him until he began shifting his weight nervously. "If even *you* now know that she will patrol the likeliest routes, surely the enemy knows it—and knowing it, will choose the least likely routes, where we will be waiting for them." He paused. "The government will dispense with your services as of this minute. I will not have anyone as demonstrably stupid offering me advice."

"But—"

"You heard me."

The aide turned and left.

"I hope there are no more like him," Tchaka announced to the room. "I think I may kill the next one."

Nobody laughed.

11.

IT WAS THREE DAYS LATER, as Tchaka held a preliminary meeting with his officers, that a Colonel Mbatha tried to kill him.

Mbatha had the computer cast a Tri-D map of the neighboring twenty light-years, perhaps five feet on a side, top and bottom, into the middle of the room. Tchaka was indicating the routes he wanted them to patrol, where he wanted them to station their ships, when Mbatha pulled out a ceramic dagger, which hadn't registered on the security devices, and tried to stab him between the shoulder blades.

I don't know how he knew it—there was no reflection in the galactic map, and Mbatha was absolutely silent—but Tchaka turned just as the colonel's hand was coming down. His own hand shot out, grabbed Mbatha by the wrist, and the two of them stood motionless for a few seconds. Then there was a loud cracking sound, Mbatha screamed, and the knife fell to the floor.

Tchaka placed his hands around Mbatha's throat, and Mbatha tried to pull his hands apart. Again, the two were motionless, this time for almost a full minute. Mbatha's eyes began bulging, and his attempts to free himself grew first more frantic, then progressively weaker. Tchaka stood still as a statue, no expression at all on his face, his fingers turning pale from the pressure he put on them. Then Mbatha went limp, and Tchaka let him fall to the floor.

He turned to another officer. "Shoot him," he said.

The man stared at him, startled, but didn't pull his laser pistol.

"He may not be dead yet," said Tchaka. "Am I expected to show him mercy so that he can try to kill me again?"

The officer withdrew his pistol, pointed it at Mbatha, but did not fire. "I think he's dead, sir. I see no sign of breathing."

Tchaka walked over, took the pistol from him, and fired a blast of solid light into the back of Mbatha's head.

"*Now* he is dead," announced Tchaka. He turned the pistol onto its owner, aimed it between his eyes, and fired again.

There was a stunned silence among the other officers.

"He would not obey me with an incapacitated enemy," said Tchaka coldly. "How could I—or you—trust him to do his duty against any enemy that was preparing to engage him in battle?" Another pause. "We will continue our briefing tomorrow."

They filed out, and he signaled me to remain behind.

"That was the second," he said when we were alone in the room.

"There was another?" I said, surprised.

"Two days ago." He seemed unconcerned. "There will be more."

"We must double—no, triple—the guard around you," I said.

He shook his head. "I am more capable of protecting myself than any half-dozen men I could assign to the task. I just want you to know that it has happened, and it will happen again."

I stared at him curiously, unable to see where this was leading.

"How many of our siblings are currently in Pretoria?" he asked.

It was not the question I was expecting. "I don't know," I said. "Maybe one, maybe two."

"Can you find the others?"

"I don't know," I replied honestly. "Some of them may not wish to be found. What do you want of them?"

"Mbatha was a Shona. The man who tried to killed me two days ago was a Swazi. I must surround myself with officers and advisors whose loyalty is unquestioned. From this day forth, every advisor, every aide, every senior officer, must be Zulu. And my siblings with be favored above all others."

"But you don't even know them!" I exclaimed, surprised. "You haven't seen most of them since we were children."

"I know that," he said calmly.

"They may not agree with your policies," I continued. "They may dislike you personally."

"I know that too."

"Then why—"

"I expected more of you, my brother," he said. "It matters nothing to me that they may hate or fear me. Before I am done, most people will either hate me or fear me, or both. But more to the point, my enemies will hate and fear those who serve me, and especially those who carry my blood in their veins. My siblings may not like me, but they will like my protection. They do not need it where they are, but once they are by my side, serving me, they will be targets, just as I am—and I will be the only thing keeping them alive. Therefore, they will serve me loyally, and do everything they can to keep me safe and in power."

It was selfish, it was savage, it was cruel…but it made sense, and I knew I would not be able to talk him out of it.

"And if some of them do not want to come?" I asked at last.

"You will explain their options, and they will come."

"Their options?"

"If they will not serve me, I have no reason to keep them alive," he replied.

And it was just as he said. Within two weeks, his entire staff was Zulu, and his closest advisors—always excepting his astrologer, Hlatshwayo—were his half-brothers and half-sisters.

12.

ANYONE WHO THOUGHT TCHAKA WOULD stay on Earth, trust his officers, and await news of the conflict in comfort and luxury clearly didn't know him.

He named his flagship *Great Elephant*, the Zulu sobriquet for the original Shaka, and it was actually the first of our fleet to take off. I was the only sibling aboard the ship, but five other brothers and sisters were on other ships as our navy entered the wormhole just beyond the Oort Cloud and emerged eighteen light-years away, precisely where Tchaka wanted us, midway on a wide arc between Delta Pavonis and DX Cancri.

As soon as we emerged and found that we were not confronting the enemy, Tchaka ordered one of his officers to pinpoint all the uninhabited oxygen worlds within five light-years of where we were.

"We might as well put the time to good use," he told me. "If we wait, sooner or later these worlds will be claimed in the name of Earth"—a contemptuous grimace—"as if Earth was a nation or a government."

Within a day the answer came back: there were seven such worlds. Tchaka immediately sent a small scout ship out to plant the flag, not of South Africa but of the Zulu nation, on each of them. It would take the better part of two months, but if we were attacked in the interim, the scout ship would be no more use to us than a lifeboat would have been to a seafaring battleship of old.

As it happens, we did not encounter the enemy for almost three months. By then we were so bored with our dull, daily routine that the presence of a small fleet of ships, doubtless carrying cargo to the embattled ships around Delta Pavonis, actually surprised us. We had almost come to the conclusion (which none dared voice) that Tchaka had guessed wrong, and that the supply lines would be established elsewhere.

"There are fourteen ships, sir," said an officer. "Shall we engage them?"

Tchaka looked at the viewscreen and frowned. "Something is wrong here," he said, more to himself than to us.

"Sir?" said the officer.

"Their configuration is wrong."

"Their formation, sir?"

He shook his head in irritation. "Their configuration."

"They are probably not human or humanoid, sir," said the officer. "Their ships will naturally be configured differently."

"Shut up," said Tchaka, still staring intently at the screen. "It's more than their configuration. There are no welds."

"What difference does that make, sir?" asked another officer.

"And the motive power," continued Tchaka. "It's wrong."

"I beg your pardon?"

Tchaka ignored him and continued staring at the screen for another full minute. Then he turned to us, the trace of a smile on his thin lips.

"We will not engage them," he announced.

"But isn't that what we came here to do?" asked the first officer.

"We will choose one ship," he continued. He turned to the officer. "I will give you the honor of selecting it. And once you do, our entire fleet will attack it with every weapon at our disposal. I want enough firepower not just to disable it but to blow it apart. Is that understood?"

"Yes, sir."

A few minutes later we closed with the enemy. Their ships tried to move into a defensive formation, but Tchaka had learned and experienced spatial warfare tactics when he served with the American fleet, and it was obvious that the cargo ship commanders had only a rudimentary knowledge of it. We managed to isolate one ship, and once we englobed it, the other thirteen ship quickly retreated.

"Now," said Tchaka, and a moment later the full firepower of our twenty ships tore the enemy ship apart.

"Spectroscope—fast!" ordered Tchaka as the ship's inner atmosphere seeped out, slowly at first, and then in a huge translucent cloud.

"They're chlorine breathers, sir," said the office manning the spectroscope.

Tchaka smiled. "I thought so. The structure was so different I had a feeling that they hadn't evolved on an oxygen world. There was no trace of welding, no indication of any science having its basis in heat or fire."

"Shall we pursue the other ships, sir?" asked an officer.

"No."

The officer looked surprised. "Sir?"

"Do you want to live on a chlorine world?" asked Tchaka. "*I* don't—and why fight for worlds we can't use? We've already found and claimed seven oxygen worlds. *That* is where our interest lies."

"But what of Earth, sir?" persisted the officer.

"What of it?" replied Tchaka with no show of concern.

The officer stared at him uncomprehendingly. "Our colonies are under attack, sir."

Tchaka shook his head. "*Earth's* colonies are under attack. As of this moment, we are no longer a part of it."

13.

Commander Sanchez sent half a dozen furious messages, all of which Tchaka ignored. Then the battle must have taken all of her attention, because the messages abruptly stopped.

Tchaka sent seven of our ships into orbit around each of the seven oxygen worlds. They reported that three were inhabited by sentient races, four were not.

"It is time to announce the founding of the Zulu Empire," he said when the last ship had sent back its information. "We will inform Earth that these worlds have acknowledged me as their *inkosi*."

"Would it not smooth the way more if they acknowledged you as their President or Premiere, rather than their king?" I asked.

"It would indeed," agreed Tchaka. Then his face hardened. "It would smooth the way if we were willing to kowtow to the wishes of America and China and the rest, if we *cared* what they thought of us, if we wanted whatever organization they have created to succeed the last in an almost endless line of failed international organizations. But we do not."

"Then, to be totally accurate, we should claim an empire of four worlds, not seven," said James Mkhize, who was not quite an aide or an advisor, though he sat in on all policy meetings. As nearly as I could tell, he had appointed himself as Tchaka's biographer, and it amused Tchaka to let him act as such.

"Seven," Tchaka replied.

"But—"

"If the original Tchaka had avoided all Shona, Mtebele, Swazi and Xhosa lands, would the first Zulu empire have ever grown beyond the size of a large farm?"

Mkhize wisely chose not to argue the point—people who argued with Tchaka tended to disappear—and asked what type of sentient life existed on the three worlds.

"I've no idea," answered Tchaka.

"Will they object to our presence?"

Tchaka seemed amused. "Does it matter?"

"No," said Mkhize quickly.

"They have not yet achieved space flight," continued Tchaka. "They will present very little problem."

"Which planet will be your headquarters?" I asked.

"I will look them over and then decide," answered Tchaka. "In the meantime, we need to populate these worlds. I have already sent word back to Pretoria that the government will pay to transport any Zulu who is willing to emigrate to any of them."

"Including the three populated worlds?" asked Mkhize.

"Of course. They will be pacified before the first Zulu colonists arrive."

And it was as Tchaka had said.

He named the seven worlds after seven Zulu kings and princes—Mpande, Cetshwayo, Dinuzulu, Mthonga, Bakuza, Jama, and Mbuyazi. It was the last three that held sentient populations. I almost said "alien populations," but of course on their worlds *we* were the aliens, not they.

The inhabitants of Bakuza were humanoid—small, quick, shaggy bipedal beings averaging less than five feet in height. They still lived in their culture's equivalent of the Stone Age. They were primarily nomadic, and they had just invented club-like weapons to bring down the herbivores that shared their planet. Arrayed against them were Tchaka's warriors, armed with laser and sonic weapons, pulse guns, and projectile weapons. We had body armor; they had none. We had rudimentary force fields to protect us from any incoming weapons; they had none. We of course had equipment that allowed us to see in the dark; they were all but blind at night.

The Battle of Bakuza took three days. The totals were staggering: four Zulus dead, three wounded; eight hundred thousand Bakuzans dead, another ninety thousand wounded.

Tchaka contacted Peter Zondo, one of our half-brothers, whom he had placed in charge of the "pacification" of Bakuza, and told him to send out parties in all directions from wherever Zondo chose to make the new capital of the planet, and elicit pledges of loyalty from the Bakuzans.

"And if any should refuse?" asked Peter.

"Kill them."

"We may need them to work the fields once we begin cultivating the planet," said Peter. "Perhaps we should invite them to—"

"*Kill them,*" repeated Tchaka, breaking the communication. He turned to an aide. "Have Captain Nene make sure he does what I have told him to do."

"And if not?"

"Kill *him*, too," said Tchaka, as if the question was too foolish to have been asked.

Jama's inhabitants were like nothing anyone had ever seen before. I'd say they looked like centaurs, but even that is misleading. They had short stubby legs, elongated bodies, narrow torsos, and heads that seemed composed entirely of wrinkles. They had no eyes, but possessed some unknown sense that functioned every bit as well, because I never saw one trip over or bump into anything. They had a complex social order, but no technology. They greeted us with open arms—well, that's a misstatement; they didn't have any arms, not by our definition—and seemed happy to give us all the land we wanted. They had no objection to being impressed into labor camps, and in fact seemed so totally lacking in resentment that many of us felt that, social order or not, they were equally lacking in sentience. After all, ants have a complex social order, and no one claims that they are sentient.

Mbuyazi was the most traditional of the three populated planets. They were humanoid, they had sophisticated weapons (though nothing to match our firepower; theirs would have been better suited for warfare in the late nineteenth or early twentieth centuries), and they had no intention of sharing their planet with anyone.

It was a bloodbath. They simply wouldn't surrender, and every adult and child fought to the death. In something under six weeks we had killed every last one of them, and even some of Tchaka's most hardened soldiers were sickened by the slaughter.

But when the dust had cleared, the Zulu Empire was in complete possession of seven worlds, and every day brought immigrants from Earth's thirty-five million Zulus to each of the worlds. Tchaka chose Cetshwayo as his headquarter world, and within a month a small city had been erected, with the Royal Palace dominating the landscape. Before long he had palatial dwellings on each of the worlds, and small cities were springing up on all of them.

We had no idea how Earth's war against the chlorine breathers was coming along, but one day we received a communication, not from Delores Sanchez but from Alexander Petrovitch, whose signature appeared over the title: "President of United Earth." He thanked us for adding seven words to the fold and announced that he would soon send his representatives out to examine them.

Tchaka responded instantly. The seven worlds—he used their new names—were part of the Zulu Empire, and were in no way connected to or under any obligation to Earth. They would pay no taxes, accept no military conscription, and would not give Earth a Most Favored trading status.

There was no answer for the next three days. We were all starting to get nervous, waiting for the other shoe to drop.

How could we have known it would be Tchaka's?

14.

EARTH ANNOUNCED THAT IT WAS considering applying economic sanctions to get Tchaka to fall in line. It insisted that the Zulu Empire agree that we were actually a series of United Earth colonies, loyal and beholden to Earth and no one else.

"What do you think?" I asked as I read the communiqués.

"They have always lacked imagination," replied Tchaka. "Even worse, they lack audacity."

He closeted himself with his military leaders and his astrologer for a long afternoon. No one else was permitted in, none of his advisors or aides knew what the conference was about, and he didn't see fit to tell us.

We found out soon enough.

Two days later one of our ships exploded halfway between Cetshwayo and Mthonga. Tchaka claimed it had been attacked by a United Earth ship and demanded reparation.

Earth denied any complicity in the incident.

"Then," announced Tchaka in a broadcast that reached not only the seven planets but Earth itself, "we shall decide upon a fitting reparation and claim it."

That night I checked the reports to find out how many of our men had been killed or wounded in the sneak attack. There were eleven names; all had been killed. But something troubled me about two of those names, and I checked further—and found that the two names I recognized, plus the other nine, had actually died in battle against the natives of Mbuyazi.

Tchaka, who rarely slept more than three or four hours a night, and was often seen wandering the halls and offices of his new headquarters in the dead of night, entered my office just as I made my discovery.

I looked up at him. "Did we really lose a ship at all?" I asked.

"Does it matter?" he replied. "We wanted an incident. Now we have one."

"*Did* we want one?"

"Absolutely."

"Why?"

He walked over to my computer and had it cast a Tri-D representation of the closest fifty light-years.

"Computer," he said, "show the worlds of the Zulu Empire in flashing yellow."

Seven worlds began flashing a bright yellow.

"Now show the colonies of United Earth in flashing blue."

Some twenty-five worlds began flashing.

He turned to me. "Why should Earth have so many while we have so few?"

"Do you actually plan to go to war with Earth?" I asked, startled.

"The first Tchaka knew better than to go to war with Britain," he replied.

"Then I don't understand."

"Britain was thousands of miles away, and was preoccupied with wars in Europe," he continued, "just as Earth is concentrating its efforts on their war with the chlorine breathers. Britain had no problem with the first Tchaka increasing the size of his territory a hundredfold, as long as he did not make war upon them."

"And Earth will let you claim parsecs upon parsecs of space, as long as you do not go to war with them or charge them for passage," I said. "But what good will it do you?"

He pointed to the half dozen colony worlds that were farthest from Earth. "Do you really think they will send any part of their fleet out to defend these worlds while they are engaged in a major war much closer to home against the chlorine breathers? What politician or general or admiral will move a single ship thirty light years from home to settle a minor dispute when the enemy they are battling is within five light years—and for all we know, maybe even closer by now?"

"So we're just going to land and claim these worlds?" I said.

"We have right on our side," he reminded me. "Earth attacked our ship, blew it up and killed the entire crew, and refuses not only to make restitution but even to acknowledge their heinous deed."

"It will never work."

He stared at me for a very long minute, and I could feel myself shrinking beneath his gaze. "Be grateful that you are my brother, and that you have served me faithfully for so long."

He turned and left my office, leaving me to consider what he had said.

I had longer to consider it than the colonists on the six worlds he claimed as reparation. The bulk of our fleet took off the next morning, and within a month all six worlds had been added—unwillingly, but unquestionably—to the Zulu Empire.

15.

TCHAKA OFTEN MADE UNANNOUNCED VISITS to the various worlds of his growing empire. I still remember the day he came back from Mpande with a new pet. It was about the size of a small dog, though it didn't resemble any dog ever whelped. It had six legs—the first animal larger than an insect I had ever seen with more than four legs. Its skin was scaly yet shiny, a brilliant red. Its head was absolutely circular, the nostrils mere slits, the ears nothing but holes. I wondered what it ate, until Tchaka fed it a small lizard. A tongue that seemed half the length of its body shot out, wrapped around the lizard, literally squeezed the life out of it in just a second or two—you could hear the tiny bones crunch from across the room—and popped it into its mouth. I guess it continued squeezing, turning everything but the bones, which it spat out a moment later, into pulp.

"I've never seen anything like it," I said. "What is it called?" I asked."

"I can't pronounce it, so I shall have to give it a name unique to itself."

"What name?"

"I will have to think about it," he said.

"Is it male or female?" I asked.

"Female."

"There are many lovely women's names," I said.

"This animal shall be our national symbol: small, unafraid, adaptable," said Tchaka. "It needs a special name."

By the next morning, he had come up with one.

"Nandi?" I repeated. "But she was the original Shaka's mother."

"The mother of the Zulu nation," he agreed. "What better name for our symbol?"

And that afternoon he designed the flag of the Zulu Empire, which displayed images of both Nandi and a Zulu spear and shield.

I had known Tchaka for most of his life, and Nandi—this bizarre alien animal—was the only living thing toward which he had ever shown affection, quite possibly because she was the only thing that had ever shown him true affection. He had always been alone, yet now Nandi was at every staff meeting, she accompanied him on every excursion to other worlds, she slept in his room, and when he addressed the Empire she was always at his side. It was if he had stored up a lifetime of affection, afraid to bestow it upon any human, and now he had found a recipient for it. No misbehavior on her part was ever punished, and every accident was forgiven.

The same could not be said for his subjects.

A single critical word against Tchaka was the equivalent of a death sentence. And like his predecessor, he didn't believe in quietly removing his enemies; he wanted potential enemies to know exactly what they could expect.

His favorite method of execution was to impale the still-living malefactor in the middle of the city square where everyone could see the punishment being carried out. Once—only once—a friend of an impaled man put him out of his agony with a burst from a laser pistol.

And two hours later, that Samaritan had replaced his friend on the cruel sharpened stake.

No one kept count—or at least no one made the count public—but in the first year of the Empire, more than a thousand men and women were sentenced to very public, very painful deaths. At the same time, our forces continued to increase in size—some thought enlistments increased primarily because able-bodied citizens felt it would get them farther away from their monarch. Yet no leader ever treated his military better than Tchaka did. The newsdisks and holos were filled with stories and holos of Tchaka, often with Nandi tucked under his arm, bestowing medals and honors upon his troops.

Earth was still fighting in its war with the chlorine breathers, who had brought allies into the battle, and neither side had any time to deal with us. We assimilated almost two or three worlds a month, and Tchaka declared our sector of space off-limits to all life forms, oxygen and chlorine breathers alike. At first neither side believed him; after we blew two or three of their ships away they got the idea.

It was after a staff meeting one morning that I found myself alone in his office with Tchaka, while Nandi perched on his desk and stared hypnotically at me as if I was her next meal.

"I have a question," he said.

"The King is allowed to ask a question," I replied.

"I gave a speech yesterday."

"I know," I said.

"I did not see you in attendance."

"You gave it in the square, surrounded by impaled corpses," I said distastefully.

"They were past objecting," he said with an amused smile. "Why do *you* object?"

"Do you know the last monarch to impale his enemies?" I said.

"The first Tchaka."

"Before that."

"Why don't you just tell me?" he said.

"Vlad Dracule," I replied. "He was known as Vlad the Impaler, and was such a monster that he served as the model for the fictional Dracula."

"What is your point?" he asked.

"Do you want to be compared to Dracula?" I said.

"Vlad lived a thousand years ago," said Tchaka, "and people still know of him. Name a single person from that century—commoner or monarch—who lived within a thousand miles of him."

And that was the end of the only discussion we ever had about impalement.

16.

ONE OF THE COLONY WORLDS Tchaka had appropriated was the agricultural world of Lincoln. They had put up some minimal resistance, but he beat it back in less than a day, installed Colonel Khuzwayo as the military governor, informed the citizens that they would be paying their taxes to the Zulu Empire rather than United Earth, and paid no more attention to it—until the day a message from Lincoln got through to Earth, complaining about the treatment the world was receiving at the hands of their governor and beseeching Earth to come to their aid.

The government of United Earth shot off a message to Tchaka, demanding that he immediately withdraw his forces and relinquish all claims to Lincoln. There was an unspoken ... *or else* at the end of it.

I was there when the message arrived. Tchaka read it, then handed it to me and told me to read it aloud, which I did.

No one knew quite how to react. No one wanted to yield to threats, but on the other hand, we didn't have the strength to fight United Earth's fleet. And of course no one dared voice an opinion for fear it would disagree with the only opinion that counted.

Tchaka waited, idly stroking Nandi, who was curled up on his desk, until he was sure no one was going to say anything.

"We have two choices," he said at last.

"Yield or fight," said an aide, nodding his head sagely.

"You are a fool," said Tchaka, "and I have no use for fools. Get out."

The aide promptly walked to the door without a word. He didn't know if he was fired or merely dismissed from the meeting, but he wasn't sentenced to death, and that was enough for the moment.

"As I was saying," continued Tchaka when the aide had gone, "we have two choices. We can ignore their message, or we can reply to it. If we ignore it, they will almost certainly send an identical message tomorrow. If we ignore it again, and continue to ignore all future messages, they will eventually send a diplomatic envoy to explain their demands. We, of course, will kill him and appropriate his ship."

He looked around the room, but no one dared show a reaction until they knew which alternative he favored.

"If, on the other hand, we choose to reply, it will be to tell them that Lincoln is under our protection, and we will take all measures necessary to protect it from United Earth's territorial aggrandizement."

"They are still preoccupied with their other military actions," offered an advisor. "They will send a few token ships."

"They will send a fleet," said Tchaka. "This is not a matter of our annexing an unpopulated world. They will not ignore an appeal for help from a former colony."

"Even if we ignore the message and they send a diplomat and we kill him, they will send a fleet anyway," said the first aide.

"And if the diplomat is sufficiently popular with the masses, they may feel compelled to send an even larger fleet," said Tchaka. "I see no purpose in delaying the inevitable."

"They may appropriate our African possessions," I pointed out.

"Only the countries we assimilated," he replied with an unconcerned shrug. "Besides, we are never going back." I could see that at least half the room wanted to suggest that a confrontation was *not* inevitable, that we could avoid it simply by giving up our claim to Lincoln, but no one dared to be the first to point it out.

Finally Tchaka spoke again.

"Have Colonel Khuzwayo contact Earth in his capacity as governor of Lincoln and tell them that their help is neither needed nor wanted."

"Yes, sir," said a military aide.

"Earth will ignore that, of course. Then we will contact them and explain that the government of Lincoln has asked for our protection against the unwanted attentions of United Earth, and we have agreed to give it to them."

As far as I could see it came to the same thing. Oh, if there'd been such a thing as a galactic court or tribunal, he could have argued that the acting government had indeed asked for his help—but we were centuries, probably millennia from galactic governments and courts. In galactic terms, we'd barely taken two steps out into our front yard.

Two hours later Colonel Khuzwayo sent the message Tchaka wanted, and that evening we received another message from Earth, threatening to send a massive fleet should the situation remain unchanged.

Tchaka warned them not to carry through with their threat, that there would be serious consequences and he would not take responsibility for them.

And that's the way it stood when a nondescript man named Dhanko Shange managed to get past Tchaka's security and bury his knife in the monarch's ribcage. It was Nandi who actually saved him, raking Shange's face with claws I didn't even know she possessed and emitting a piercing scream that brought help on the run.

They killed Shange on the spot and rushed Tchaka to the hospital, while he complained all the way, not of his pain, but rather that they hadn't left Shange alive so he could be impaled and left on public display for his crime. There was no serious internal damage, and Tchaka was released two days later. His first official act was to name Nandi the governor of

Cetshwayo. Everyone thought it was crazy; no one dared say a word in protest.

Three days later we got word that a massive fleet had taken off from Earth and was headed in the direction of the Zulu Empire.

"They are fools," said Tchaka. "They think I am bluffing. They will learn that I never bluff."

Ten minutes later he ordered Colonel Khuzwayo to evacuate all military personnel from Lincoln. When Khuzwayo reported two hours later that it had been accomplished, he gave orders to destroy the planet.

"Do you mean to destroy all human life on it?" came the message from Khuzwayo.

"Blow it up," answered Tchaka. "The bigger the explosion, the better."

I could see the same thought reflected on every face in the room: *Now he's done it! Earth will have to avenge this. We are all walking dead men.*

And finally a few of them, convinced that their doom was imminent, found their voices.

"They have to have seen that," said one aide.

"I certainly hope so," said Tchaka.

"Earth will kill us now."

"Earth will leave us alone now," said Tchaka easily.

"After what we did?" said another man incredulously.

"I have sent a private communication to the President of United Earth, with a copy to the commander of the approaching fleet."

All eyes turned to him.

"The gist of it is that we have twenty-four more former colonies," said Tchaka, "and I will destroy one for every light-year closer they approach. Lincoln was merely a demonstration."

And even as the words left his mouth, we received a coded message that Earth had withdrawn its fleet.

17.

I HAD JUST FINISHED SHAVING and was preparing to go to bed when there was a knock at my door. I knew it wasn't Tchaka, for if he wanted to speak with me he would send an underling to bring me to him. I also knew it wasn't a thief—they don't announce their presence by knocking—but I couldn't think of who would want to speak to me an hour after midnight.

"Come in," I said.

The door opened, and Peter Zondo and three more of my half-siblings—a man and two women—entered my quarters.

"What can I do for you?" I asked.

Peter put his finger to his lips, waited for the door to close, then nodded to the two women—Sarah Khubeka and Bettina Cele—who produced small glowing instruments and began scanning for hidden holo cameras and listening devices, while the man, Joseph Thabethe, trained a laser pistol on the door. Finally they finished and nodded to him.

"It is safe," said Sarah, though Joseph kept his weapon out.

I was pretty sure I knew what was coming next, but I waited for Peter to speak.

"We must stop him," he said.

"How?" I asked. "Professional assassins have tried. They are all either dead and buried, or dying and on public display."

"He is out of control," persisted Peter. "He destroyed an entire planet—a planet filled with human beings."

"And he's killed enough others to populate a colony world," added Bettina.

"He is *not* out of control," I replied. "He is in complete, total control of his empire."

"He is a monster!" said Bettina.

"I am not denying that," I said. "If he wasn't one to begin with, he has become one."

"Well, then?" demanded Peter.

"Most of the people worship him," I said. "But each day more and more of them hate and fear him."

"You are making our point."

I shook my head. "They also hate and fear those who serve him. They hate the military and the police—and most of all, they hate his brothers and sisters, who have been elevated to positions of authority." I stared at the four of them. "He is all that is keeping us alive."

"I am willing to trade my life for his," said Sarah. "I loathe him! I never wanted to be brought here in the first place. I was literally kidnapped from my home in Durban in the middle of the night."

"He knows you hate him," Peter said to her. "He will never give you the opportunity to kill him." There was a long, pregnant pause. "It must be you, John," he continued, turning to me. "You have been with him the longest. He is often alone with you. You have his confidence." Another pause. "You must be the one to do it."

"No one and nothing has his confidence except Nandi," I said. "He would know the moment I approached him. He knows my mind better than I do. I could not hide it from him."

"Nonsense," said Peter. "All it takes is self-control."

"Even if I could get near him without his knowing what I had in mind, he is a force of nature," I said. "I cannot defeat him."

"You mean you *will* not," he said angrily.

I shook my head. "I mean I *cannot*."

"Then *I* will," said Sarah. She turned and stalked out of the room, followed by Joseph and Bettina.

"She will fail," I said.

"Probably," agreed Peter. "But at least she is not afraid to try."

"She will be just as dead."

"Is that all you have to say?" demanded Peter.

"What do you *want* me to say?" I replied.

"That it is time to be rid of him."

"He is a monster," I said. "I told you that. I disagree with his methods. You know that too." I paused uncomfortably. "But we were nothing for half a millennium, and in a tiny handful of years he has given us an empire."

"We do not need one," said Peter firmly.

"You do not understand," I said.

"Enlighten me."

"You know how many enemies the Zulus made building this empire, how many people we killed, how many governments we threatened and humiliated," I said. "What will happen to us if we lose it?"

He seemed about to argue the point, then turned abruptly and walked out.

Nothing untoward happened the next two days, and I decided Sarah had thought better of it. Tchaka was preoccupied with reports that there were sentient beings on the fourth planet circling Epsilon Indi, and he had decided that it was in the Empire's best interest to form an alliance with any race that was not yet allied with Earth.

He spent hours with Hlatshwayo as the astrologer studied the solar alignments (which struck me as ridiculous, since we were no longer within twenty light-years of the Earth's solar system) and cast a number of horoscopes. Finally he determined that Morgan Raziya, another half-brother, should be the one to make contact with Epsilon Indi IV. Tchaka consented, but he didn't have much faith in Morgan's abilities, or anything else about him except his paternal bloodline, and he decided to send four well-armed ships with him, rather than a single, unarmed, non-threatening diplomatic ship.

"This is our first true step into the galaxy, John," he said to me after Hlatshwayo had left. He paused to pet Nandi, who had been sitting on his lap for the past half hour. "Perhaps," he said to her, "I shall make you the Queen of the entire Indi system." He turned to me. "What would you think of that, my brother?"

The quickest way to assure a painful death was to tell exactly what I thought of it. "I fear she may have some difficulty communicating with her staff," I said carefully.

Tchaka chuckled in amusement. "It might keep them on their toes, considering the consequences." He planted a kiss on Nandi's round face. "She has never had any trouble making her wishes known to me."

I must have been feeling exceptionally bold, because I replied: "Perhaps that is because she does not speak to you on matters of policy."

He stared at me, and for a moment I thought I had gone too far, but eventually he went back to petting Nandi and discussing his plans for expanding the empire.

I dined alone, as usual, went back to my quarters, and watched a holo until I fell asleep. I was up at sunrise, as usual, and a few minutes later I began making my way to my office.

There were three new stakes in front of the Royal Palace. Skewered on one of them was the barely-breathing Sarah Khubeka. The other two were empty.

I walked by my office and went directly to Tchaka's, where I found two of his elite security team standing at attention in front of him. Finally he nodded to two more guards, who marched them out at gunpoint.

"What happened?" I asked.

"My sister—the one from Durban—tried to kill me last night."

"I saw her as I arrived," I said.

"The two men you saw just now had found out what she planned and warned me." He smiled a humorless smile. "I made sure I was wearing my ceremonial robes, with my body armor hidden beneath it. She fired two bullets and one laser burst into it before I took her weapons away from her and turned her over to my bodyguards."

"If they warned you, why were they being taken out at gunpoint?"

"They are to be impaled on each side of her," said Tchaka. "Surely you saw the empty stakes."

"But if their information saved your life…" I began, puzzled.

It is because of them that I must kill my sister!" he yelled, his face contorted in fury.

I suddenly found myself looking back on what I had said to Peter Zondo and thinking that there was very little a hostile galaxy could do to us that Tchaka wouldn't do first.

18.

THE EMPIRE GREW. WE ADDED four more new worlds in the next half year, and Earth remained preoccupied with more immediate threats. Tchaka kept building the military against the day that Earth was finally able to concentrate on the upstart Zulu Empire, but that day seemed to keep receding into the future.

The colony worlds thrived under his firm rule. There were no jobless, no homeless; if a man couldn't find gainful employment elsewhere, he was transferred to the nearest farm on the nearest world. We tried to establish a market for our goods among Earth's enemies, but being aliens—and some were very alien indeed—they had scant use for most of the items we wished to sell or trade. This caused Tchaka to send us further afield, spreading our population to still more uninhabited worlds that would need our goods.

The alien races did want something a few of our mining worlds possessed: fissionable materials. But that was the one thing Tchaka wouldn't trade or sell them, on the reasonable assumption that the alien worlds were clearly not trading for a planetary power source. That meant they wanted the materials for weapons or to power their ships, and those were two advantages he had no intention of giving them.

He began taking walks around the centers of whatever cities he was visiting on his worlds, always accompanied by half a dozen bodyguards, and of course by Nandi. If one did not know better, he almost looked like a man taking his pet out for a walk—except that Nandi had never worn a leash in her life, looked like no other pet in the whole of human history, and far from being merely a pet, she was officially the Queen of the Epsilon Indi and the Delta Pavonis systems. Tchaka always had a small lizard or two in his pocket or the folds of his ceremonial robes, and delighted in tossing them in the air and seeing her tongue shoot out and wrap itself around them on the way down.

I still remember the first time she missed. We were inspecting a new barracks just outside the town of Bhebhe on the new colony world of Dingiswayo. As we reached the end of the building, Tchaka produced a small lizard, no more than six inches in length except for the tail, and flipped it in the air. Nandi's tongue shot out—and she missed it by a good two inches.

I laughed, but cut my laughter short when Tchaka glared furiously with me. He picked Nandi up and cradled her body in his arms, a worried expression on his face.

"She must be ill," he said.

"Everyone's allowed to miss once in a while," I said. "Even her. Even you."

"No," he said. "She is perfection. If she missed, something has to be wrong with her."

"I suppose we can take her to a veterinarian," I suggested.

"Our veterinarians can only treat mutated cattle," he said. "None of them has ever examined a member of Nandi's species. I do not think it even has a name." He put her down on the ground and walked a few feet away. She followed him, but she didn't have the usual spring to her step. "This inspection is ended. We're going back to Cetshwayo."

And twenty minutes later our ship took off.

I didn't think there was anything seriously wrong with Nandi. I thought that she may have had a mild stomach ache, or perhaps the atmosphere or gravity on Dingiswayo was not quite what she was used to, but I assumed she'd be fine again in another day or two.

Once we landed, Tchaka took her back to his office, where she spent most of her time, in the hope that familiar surroundings would somehow cure whatever ailed her. She didn't get any worse, but she didn't get any better. He sent half a dozen men out to find the tastiest lizards and bring them back, he collected piles of silks and made beds in every corner of the office, but she preferred sleeping on his desk, as she always had.

The next day he tossed a couple of lizards in her direction, and she totally ignored them.

He turned to his assembled aides. "Out!" he commanded. "She needs rest, not distractions."

"But Tchaka, we have an empire to run, business to transact," said one of them.

I thought he might kill the man on the spot, but he was so concerned with Nandi that he merely pointed to the door, and one by one we filed out.

I had been with him longer than anyone. I had never seen him show sympathy or concern for a friend, for a sibling, for anyone or anything—until now. I was the last to leave the office, and as I turned back I saw him holding this alien creature more tenderly, more lovingly, than any human parent has ever held a baby.

"It is sick," an aide whispered to me as we walked down the long hallway. "An entire empire's business is on hold because a totally worthless pet may or may not have a stomach ache."

"It shows he is a leader with great compassion," said another.

"And when we walk out the front door," said the first aide, "you will pass a hundred examples of his compassion."

"They were enemies of the state," said the second.

"And is that ugly *thing* a friend of the state?"

"She is a friend of Tchaka's," I said. "His *only* friend. I would be very careful what I said of her." I was going to add the old adage about the walls having ears, but he looked at me with such sudden terror in his eyes that I realized he was thinking only of *my* ears—and my mouth.

"I did not mean—" he began quickly.

"It's all right," I said. "I'm a brother, not an informant."

He thanked me, but he also managed to get out of my presence as quickly as he could.

I went to a local restaurant, and while I was seated at a table, waiting to be served, I was joined by Peter Zondo.

"Is what I heard true?" he asked.

"Probably," I said. "But suppose you tell me what you heard anyway?"

"The Princess—or is she the Empress?—didn't eat her breakfast, and the universe has come to a stop."

I was about to tell him not to be so sarcastic—but then I realized that he had properly assessed the situation, at least in regard to *our* universe.

"It is true," I said at last.

"Ten thousand women throw themselves at him, and he saves his affection for *that*," he continued contemptuously. "The man is sicker than his pet."

"What do you want me to say?" I replied irritably. "That at least he cares for something?"

"You know what I want you to say—and to *do*," said Peter.

"What do you think will happen if someone—not me, but someone—killed him?" I asked.

"We would be free of a tyrant," he said, puzzled by my question.

"How do you know that the man who killed him, the man who *could* kill him, would not be an even greater tyrant?"

"There *are* no greater tyrants!" said Peter passionately.

"There have been," I said. "Caligula, Stalin—"

"And Rome and Russia and Brazil and New Zealand all survived them!" he interrupted.

"Keep your voice down," I cautioned him.

"You see?" he said. "We are his brothers, his most trusted advisors—and we dare not speak our minds in public."

"You are welcome to speak your mind," I said, becoming annoyed with him. "Just don't speak it at my table."

He held his hands up, as if to cut off the conversation. He lowered his head in thought for a moment, and finally looked up at me. "If you will not do what we have discussed in the past, will you at least consider one other thing?"

"Probably not," I said.

"Do you not even wish to know what it is?"

"You're going to tell me whether I ask or not."

He learned forward and lowered his voice until no one else could hear it. "Kill Nandi," he hissed.

I just stared at him.

"Maybe it will bring him to his senses," he continued.

"You mean the way he was before he found Nandi?" I replied sardonically.

He got to his feet. "You are hopeless," he said contemptuously, and walked out of the restaurant without another word.

Late that night I found myself too restless to sleep, so I decided to take a walk. Eventually I wound up in front of the Royal Palace, and I could see the light on in Tchaka's suite of rooms. He had never had any trouble sleeping, and I knew he was sitting up with Nandi, trying to make her comfortable.

I should have kept walking or returned home, but instead I remained looking up at his room for another ten minutes. Then, just as I was about to finally leave, the night air was broken by the most agonized, heartbroken scream I have ever heard in my life.

It did not come from Nandi.

Well, at least that's over with, I thought.

But I was wrong. It was just beginning.

19.

NANDI WAS GIVEN A ROYAL funeral with full military honors. British monarchs never received a more formal send-off. She was wrapped in the flag that bore her likeness, then placed in a small golden casket, which was carried to her tomb—an indoor mausoleum in one corner of Tchka's office—by four large soldiers.

But before she was brought to her final resting place, Tchaka announced that he would speak at the funeral. There were perhaps five thousand people in attendance, most of them doubtless feeling slightly ridiculous as I myself did. I kept wondering what he was going to say, for the Zulus do not speak over their dead.

Finally he stepped forward, and all eyes turned to him.

"Cetshwayo has lost its queen, and the Zulu Empire has lost its empress," he said, and I was struck by the fact that no one dared to even smile, let alone laugh. "This is the greatest tragedy to befall us since we left the Earth," he continued, "and I hereby declare a mourning period to last until one year from today. This period will be observed on every planet and by every citizen of the Empire, no matter how far-flung."

Then, as the crowd was about to relax and begin dispersing, he spoke again. "For one year, no member of the Empire will imbibe in any intoxicants. No one will take any stimulants. No one will indulge in any sexual relations." A brief pause. "I will not permit these guidelines to be ignored."

Then he turned and entered the Palace, followed by the four men bearing Nandi's casket.

There was an immediate troubled buzzing among the attendees. Did he mean it? A whole year? Just us, or every world? Married citizens too? A hundred worried questions, a few disbelieving remarks, and finally the crowd dispersed.

An hour later I was summoned to Tchaka's office, along with most of my half-siblings. If he had been crying, there was no trace of it.

"I *will* enforce the period of mourning," was his way of greeting us.

"It may turn the people against you," said Bettina.

"Then we will have to find work to keep them busy, won't we?" he replied coldly. He looked at each of us in turn, then stopped when he came to Peter Zondo. "Peter, you look unhappy."

"I am unhappy that Nandi has died," replied Peter carefully.

"Do not lie to me," said Tchaka severely. "You have a problem. Tell me what it is."

"I have mourned the passing of loved ones before," said Peter. "So has everyone else. But I cannot recall anyone ever abstaining from all pleasure for an entire year as a sign of mourning."

"It happened once before," replied Tchaka.

There was a long uneasy silence. It was obvious Tchaka was waiting for Peter to ask the question, and finally he did: "When?"

"When Nandi died."

"But she just died yesterday," said Peter with a frown. "I do not understand."

"Not *this* Nandi," was the reply. "Nandi, the mother of the first Tchaka. That is what gave me the idea."

"It is a dangerous idea," said Peter. "There are certain things the people will not put up with."

"There is only one thing," answered Tchaka with absolute certainty. "Weakness." He suddenly turned to me. "Do you agree, John?"

"Ask me in six months," I said.

"They are all cattle," he said. "In this entire empire, there is only one bull." He stared at us contemptuously. "You will want to indulge in sex, but you won't. You will want to drink beer or liquor, but you will think twice about it and decide not to. You want to kill me, but you haven't the courage." He turned his back to us. "You wish a target? Here it is." He stood motionless for almost a minute. "No? I thought not." He pivoted to once again face us. "Get out of here. You are desecrating Nandi's resting place by your presence."

As we left, Peter leaned over to me. *"Now?"* he whispered.

"He turned his back on you for a full minute," I said. "Why didn't you take advantage of it?"

"I didn't have a weapon," he said uncomfortably.

I grabbed him by his shoulder, spun him around, and reached for the knife handle that was just visible above the top of his belt. I got my hands on it and pulled it out.

"For shaving?" I asked dryly.

He glared at me and said nothing.

"You are everything he thinks you are," I said, handing him back the dagger.

"Do you think you're any better?" he said bitterly.

"I have never claimed to be," I answered.

"We will both regret not taking advantage of the opportunity he gave us tonight," said Peter.

"It's possible," I admitted.

"You take no drugs and you have no wife," he said accusingly. "You cannot know what this will mean to us."

"Go away until you have something intelligent to say," I told him.

"We cannot let this happen," he persisted.

"And if we do not let it happen, who will replace him? You?"

"Why not?"

"Go away," I repeated. "I prefer the half of my blood that I do not share with you."

He glared hatefully at me, but finally turned and walked off. I had no desire to remain in my siblings' company. I walked the streets alone for perhaps an hour, then went to my apartment. Tchaka hadn't mentioned a ban on holos, so I watched a mindless entertainment for a couple of hours, then began preparing for bed. Suddenly I became aware that I was not alone any longer. I turned and found myself facing Tchaka.

"I thought I locked the door," I said.

"No door can keep me out," he said, without explaining how he had gained entrance.

"Why are you here?"

"I have a question, my brother," said Tchaka.

"I am your servant," I replied. "You have but to ask."

"I know they want me dead, my half-brothers and half-sisters," he said. "They are fools, for once I am dead they are next. And I knew when I turned my back that none of them, not Peter, not Joseph, not any of them, would have the courage to put a blade or a bullet between my shoulders." He paused and stared at me. "You are not much of a man," he said, "but you are better than they are. Why did you not kill me?"

"Seriously?" I said.

"It is a serious question."

"I do not know if what comes after you will be any better," I replied.

He looked into my eyes. "I believe you." He walked to the door, opened it, and turned back to me. "It won't be, you know," he said, and then he was gone.

20.

For a month after Nandi's death no one took Tchaka's edict seriously. Most of them, especially the ones who didn't live on Cetshwayo or hadn't seen him with Nandi, felt it was like the behavior of a man who'd lost a beloved dog or cat, a momentary emotional aberration but something he would soon get over. You didn't stop drinking or going to bed with your spouse because a man's pet had died six or eight star systems away.

After two months, they knew better. Villages and cities were raided in the middle of the night, and offenders killed on the spot, or else dragged off to be impaled. Restaurants that tried to sell beer or wine under the table were burned to the ground, their owners killed.

Mthonga's climate was ideal for growing everything, including marijuana and poppies. Initially Tchaka ordered his army to destroy the offending fields. When more sprang up, he did to that world what he had done to Lincoln—he had it blown apart.

The people began walking around hunched over, staring into shadows, jumping at the slightest sounds. Everyone eyed their neighbors suspiciously. Tchaka received an average of three petitions a week to terminate the mourning period. He adamantly refused.

"I have not enjoyed my life since Nandi died," he said to me one morning after tearing up yet another petition. "Why should they?"

The answer was obvious, but quite beyond his ability to see.

Four months passed, then five, then six—and now a new horror arose, for women who had become pregnant since Nandi's death were showing the signs of it, and they and their husbands were killed on the spot. Soon no pregnant woman would leave her house. The soldiers began following lone male shoppers home, and when they found a woman with child, she and her mate would be killed instantly or sometimes impaled side by side.

Worlds began to resemble death camps. No one looked right or left, no one laughed, no one spoke. Even if Tchaka was a dozen worlds away, even if he had never set foot on a particular planet, that didn't mean his army, his spies, and his informers weren't watching everyone.

The only hope of the citizenry was that word of what was happening would reach Earth, though I don't know what they thought Earth could do about it. Not only was Earth still spread thin throughout the Spiral Arm, engaged in half a dozen conflicts with alien races, but it was clear to those of us who knew him best that Tchaka would destroy an entire world before he would allow it to resist his rule. After all, he had done it twice already.

One of our half-sisters, Miriam Zuma, became pregnant. Tchaka strangled her with his own hands. A brother, Jacob Nzama, tried to steal a ship and flee from Cetshwayo; Tchaka killed him too.

"There are only four of his half-brothers and half-sisters left, brother," said Peter Zondo when he accosted me outside the Royal Palace. "He means to kill us all. The man is in love with Death."

"The man is not in love with anyone or anything," I replied. "The only thing he ever cared for is dead."

"Fifty thousand of *us* are dead too," said Peter bitterly.

"They broke his rules."

"They have no contract with him," said Peter. "They didn't vote for him. They did not ask for their worlds to be assimilated into this hideous Zulu Empire."

"The mourning period is half over," I said.

"So he will only destroy one more planet and kill fifty thousand more men and women?" snapped Peter. "That's the good news, is it?"

I had no answer.

"And what of next year?" continued Peter. "If he gets an upset stomach, will the consumption of meat be forbidden for a year? If he has a cavity, will every citizen's teeth be pulled?"

"You're being nonsensical," I said.

"Am I, John?" he replied. "Look around you, and tell me anything anyone could say would be more nonsensical than this." He looked around to make sure we were still alone, then lowered his voice. "Tonight," he whispered. I merely stared at him. "I will do it tonight. We can wait no longer."

"Will you have help?"

He shook his head. "No. I'll be alone—and if you tell him you're a dead man." He made a face. "Hell, if I don't do it, we're all dead men anyway." He looked around once more—a habit most of us had picked up since Nandi's death—and then turned back to me. "Aren't you going to wish me luck?"

"I wish you life," I said.

But I knew it was a futile wish.

21.

I saw Peter Zondo's corpse the next morning. It still clutched a laser pistol in its hand, but the hand had been literally squeezed to a pulp by a larger, far stronger hand. You would literally have had to cut the formless flesh away with a knife to free the pistol.

There were very few marks of violence on the body. My guess was that he'd been killed by a blade or a bullet through the back of his shirt. Clearly he'd never gotten a shot off. As I reconstructed it, Tchaka must have known he was coming, must have followed his approach through the various security devices. Probably he inserted infrared lenses in his eye, turned off the lights, kept the approach to his room very bright, and simply waited for Peter to open the door and enter. He'd have grabbed Peter's hand, ground it to a shapeless blob with his own massive hand, then killed him at his leisure. Of course, I could be totally wrong. It is possible that Peter had never gotten near Tchaka's private quarters and the security force had killed him…but I wouldn't bet on it.

I was summoned to Tchaka's office that afternoon.

"Did you see our half-brother?" he asked.

"It's hard to miss him," I said distastefully. "He's very prominently displayed."

"He was a fool."

"Probably," I agreed.

He stared at me. "You have been with me the longest, John. I know you bear me no love, but you have always known where your best interest lies."

I made no answer, because I couldn't see what he was leading up to.

"And because you know where your best interest lies," he continued, "and because our fates are interlinked, you are the one man I can trust."

I simply looked at him, waiting for whatever came next.

"I have a confession to make, John."

"Oh?" I said.

Most people seem uncomfortable when they make a confession. Tchaka was not most people.

"I indulged in a momentary weakness some months ago," he began.

"A momentary weakness?" I repeated, frowning.

He nodded his head. "And as a result, there is a girl in a room down the corridor, a girl no one but myself has seen for ten weeks now, who is visibly pregnant."

I stared at him, but said nothing.

"Clearly I cannot execute myself," he continued. "The Empire must have an emperor, and no one else is remotely fit for the position. But given that I have ordered the death of every other pregnant woman, I cannot have her seen in her condition."

"You've hidden her pretty well so far," I said.

"She will have the baby two months before the year is up—and *that* I cannot keep a secret, or at least I cannot be sure of keeping it a secret."

"You're going to kill her," I said dully.

"No, John," he replied. "*You're* going to kill her."

"I've never killed anybody," I protested.

"Then it's time you learned," said Tchaka. "I have no compunction about killing her. But I have never sired a child, and probably will never sire another. I would prefer that you kill it." He shot me a self-deprecating smile. "You see, John? I am capable of human emotions after all."

"Let her live," I said. "This isn't her fault."

"She dies," he said firmly, opening a drawer of his desk and withdrawing a small pistol.

"Has she any family?" I asked as he handed me the gun.

"Not any more."

"How old is she?"

He shrugged. "Thirteen, fourteen, something like that."

"I have one question," I said. "What would have happened to her all those months ago if she had obeyed your mourning edict and refused to sleep with you?"

"I would probably have raped her," he said matter-of-factly, "and I would certainly have killed her afterward for refusing me."

I stared at him for a long moment. "It won't be worse," I said at last.

"What won't be worse?" he asked curiously.

"Whatever replaces you," I said, pointing the pistol at his chest.

He glared furiously at me. "Make the first shot count, John," he said. "You'll never get another."

I pulled the trigger.

He fell back against the wall, an expression of surprise on his face. I fired twice more, but with no effect. I knew I had hit him. I heard the *thunk* of the bullets as they dug into him. Then I remembered that he was wearing body armor, and I aimed at his head.

"At last, you are finally my brother," he said, just before I pulled the trigger.

22.

And that is the story—or at least the story so far.

When news of Tchaka's death spread throughout the Empire, world after world declared its independence. I can foresee the day, maybe thirty years from now, maybe even less, when the Zulus will be confined to this world, perhaps to just a small section of it.

And, as before, they will look at each newborn boy and ask: are you the One? Could you possibly be the One?

I pray that the answer will always be No.

EPILOGUE

AFTER MAKING THE ZULUS THE dominant tribe in all of Africa and expanding his kingdom to the point where he controlled an area larger than France, Shaka was assassinated by his half-brother Dingane.

With the death of Shaka, the Zulus fell from primacy for the next five hundred years.